December 1993

PERDITA

She didn't know her name, where she had come from, or how old she was. She had been discovered nearly half dead at the bottom of a well and brought to a convent to recover. The doctor guessed she was about seventeen —and the nurse named her Perdita.

Gradually Perdita regained her physical strength, but not her memory. She felt increasingly drawn to a nearby horse farm and took a job there, discovering to her surprise that she was an excellent horsewoman.

As she prepared to ride in a local horse show, however, her menacing past began to unfold —in frightening and elusive ways.

PERDITA

PERDITA

by
Isabelle Holland

MAGNA PRINT BOOKS
Long Preston, North Yorkshire,
England.

British Library Cataloguing in Publication Data.

Holland, Isabelle, *1920—*
    Perdita.
    I. Title
    813'.54 (F)

    ISBN 1-85057-576-2
    ISBN 1-85057-577-0 pbk

First Published in Great Britain by Severn House Publishers
Ltd., 1987.

Published in Large Print 1989 by arrangement with Severn
House Publishers Ltd., London and Little, Brown and Company
Inc., New York.

Printed and bound in Great Britain by
Redwood Burn Limited, Trowbridge, Wiltshire.

I would like to thank Donna Mihalik of Princeton, New Jersey, for her technical advice concerning the training of horses and their riders. Needless to say, any mistakes are mine.

CHAPTER ONE

It was the sight of the horses that did it. Sister Bede and I were driving in the convent jeep between the lush green fields where, behind their white fences, horses were grazing.

'Whose farm is that?' I said, surprising myself a little by my interest, except, of course, that these days everything and nothing was a surprise.

Sister Bede glanced to the side. 'Stanton Farm, I think.'

At the other end of the far field two riders jumped the gate and cantered across. Given the blonde ponytail under the riding helmet the lead rider appeared to be female. The horseman behind was bareheaded and dark. Both were good riders.

'They ride well,' I said idly.

The sister glanced at me. 'You seem to know something about riding,' she said with a slight smile.

'I do, don't I?'

It was strange, these discoveries. More than strange. But I had come to expect them. Once,

Sister Bede (who was more or less the convent chauffeur, since no one else could handle the jeep) and I were driving past a dusty park outside the nearest town. Some young kids were playing baseball. Sister Bede slowed the jeep so she could watch. I watched too, bored and uncomprehending. A boy holding a bat was trying to hit a ball.

'*Strrrike!*' The dignified young nun beside me yelled suddenly. Then when I jumped, said, 'Sorry, I didn't mean to startle you. But the ball caught the inside corner.'

'You must know baseball.'

She sighed, then laughed. 'That was always my second vocation.'

'I don't,' I said. And knew that it was true. I simply didn't know what those children were doing, jumping up and down and yelling on their positions of a rough square. And—no feeling came with my recognition that I knew nothing. It was a conclusion that was blessedly neutral.

In the previous seven months, which was all I knew of my life, I had learned that I had no idea how to cook, could read French, could play the piano, could not play the guitar, talked the kind of Northeastern American that could not be localized more narrowly than that, that I had an aversion to crowds, but knew my

10

way around the New York subway system, could ride a bike, would not under any circumstances eat green beans and, now, after my comment about the riders, that I knew the difference between those who rode poorly and those who rode well.

The important things I did not know were: my name, where I had spent my life until seven months ago, with whom, where I came from, whom I belonged to (if anyone), how old I was.

At the convent, to whose sanatorium I had been taken after being found at the bottom of a nearby dry well, I was known as Perdita. Perdita, meaning lost. Because when I had waked up in one of the sanatorium beds seven months previously, I discovered that I had lost my memory, which meant that I had lost myself.

Considering how far I had fallen down that well I was extraordinarily lucky. I had broken my head, my shoulder and my leg, and had, in addition, multiple bruises and contusions, two cracked ribs and concussion.

The nuns were of a nursing order, so Dr Pusey and Reverend Mother Julian decided to keep me there. My clothes—jeans, shirt, sneakers, bra and underpants—bore the labels of garments sold in any department store from coast to coast. In one jeans pocket there were some crumpled tissues. In the other, one dollar

11

and thirty-seven cents. And that was all. I wore no jewellery. There was nothing whatsoever to identify me in any way.

As time passed, the police were queried as to any missing persons who fit my description. That was when I learned that countless teenagers—literally thousands—ranging from thirteen to eighteen had been reported missing at about the time I was found. Understandably, the authorities and parents were most concerned about the adolescents at the younger end of that age range. At eighteen years old the teenager is an adult. She could still be missing. She could still have a frantic family. But the sense of urgency or perhaps fear is greater with the sixteen-year-old, and even more with fourteen and thirteen.

'How old do you think I am?' I asked Dr Pusey once.

'Seventeen, maybe eighteen.'

Out of bed by that time, I stared at myself in the mirror. The jeans and shirt were now loose. Medium height, narrow body, short brown curly hair, greenish eyes, acceptable features. Seventeen or eighteen felt right—how or why I didn't know. Then I wondered, supposing he had said twenty-five? Would it have felt *not* right? That was one of the times that panic had swept over me, making me feel a little sick.

Because if Dr Pusey had looked up over his black bag in the same speculative way and said, 'About twenty-five,' I was afraid I might have found it just as acceptable.

I did not want to leave the convent. That fact surfaced when one of the several neurologists and psychologists I'd been taken to see said, casually, 'What are you going to do when you leave?'

Big claws seemed to close around my stomach. 'Leave where?'

'The convent.' The psychologist stared at me across her desk. 'You're not thinking of staying there and becoming a nun or anything, are you?'

'No!' It was not difficult to answer that. I had no desire to become a nun. But there was no denying the terror that gripped me when I considered walking out of the only haven I knew, into a world I didn't know, and which was holding secrets about myself I didn't share.'

The psychologist looked at me in a kindly way. 'You don't like the idea of leaving, do you?'

'No.' For some reason, though I couldn't have said why, I also didn't like the psychologist. It wasn't that she was unkind. But she made me feel...uncomfortable. I wanted very much to leave and not come back. So much so, in fact—I got to my feet. 'I must go now.' I picked up the little handbag I'd bought with some of the money the nuns had given me to buy something other than my jeans and shirt to wear. The psychologist was still talking as I left the room.

Reverend Mother Julian would not force me to leave. I knew that and was grateful. 'On the other hand,' she said. 'You should get some kind of a job. I don't think hiding here is going to restore what you've lost.'

'Do you think I'll ever remember?'

'Yes.'

I smiled at the nun with the kind eyes and the brusque manner.

She went on, 'I know that I'm treading where angels fear to. No doctor is going to walk out on that particular limb. But I feel quite sure you will.'

Her statement might have been unscientific, but it comforted me. Not knowing who I was made me feel amputated, cut off, in the most desolate sense of the word—lost. I did not want to go through life like that.

Yet one of the doctors had said to me, 'We can't be sure, of course. And you certainly had a nasty blow on the head. But part of your amnesia could be psychologically induced—or at least retained. You could be blocking something that you don't want to face—that you find frightening.'

Somehow that upset me more. 'But I was concussed! You said so.'

'No question! But, physiologically speaking, there is no reason why your memory should not be starting to come back. Has any of it at all returned? No flickers or flashes—even if they last only seconds?'

'No.' But my answer didn't come immediately.

'You hesitated.'

'I have dreams.'

'Do you know what they are?'

I shook my head, and felt the first warning pain flickering through my skull. I knew that I was beginning a blinder—my nickname for the only other remaining legacy of whatever it was that had happened to me. I called them blinders because, among other things, they literally blinded me for a while—sometimes minutes, sometimes hours—and as long as they lasted, they tore at me with a savagery that left me sweating and nauseated. Nothing did any good. Fighting the pain, resisting it, made it worse. I learned it was better to accept the pain, plunge into the centre of it and surrender to it. In some way that took away the terrible power of the pain. So I simply lived through them, lying in my darkened room until the worst had passed and the pain receded to the ordinary headache, which normal people had and for which they took two aspirin.

'Are you getting a headache?' the doctor asked sharply.

I nodded, then stopped. It made the pain much worse. 'Yes,' I said.

'I don't want to get you hooked on narcotics,' the doctor said, 'which is why I don't give you a prescription. But take these aspirin.'

I took them and crept out to the jeep where Sister Bede was waiting. After one glance at me, she drove back to the convent as gently as possible. That blinder lasted until evening.

But not everything was downbeat. My memory didn't return, I still couldn't recall dreams. But the blinders started coming less often. Perhaps that was why Reverend Mother began gently prodding me about doing something outside the convent.

'You're trying to get rid of me,' I said, fully aware that it was not true.

'You know that's just rubbish.' Reverend Mother was English, and for reasons I of course did not know, I found the crisp, English sound of her voice reassuring. 'You're welcome to stay here as long as you like,' she went on. 'And you must certainly consider it your haven to come back to if you do get a job. I'm just not convinced that you're going to get better sitting around here putting our files in order and retyping some of our records—nice as it is to have it done.' Because I had begun to work in her office after I discovered that (a) I was beginning to be bored, and (b) I could type, although not very well.

The trouble was, if I took a job elsewhere, it would be almost impossible for me to live at the convent, which was in the country. The bus service to the town was not such that it could be relied on to get me to a job and back again, and I couldn't expect to be driven there daily and then picked up.

'I don't suppose you have any feeling that you were in school or college?' Sister Mary Helen said to me once. She was the librarian, and something of a scholar. She had once been librarian in a famous convent school, but had come here to this convent when her arthritis had made it difficult for her to get around. She spoke to me hopefully.

I grinned. 'Are you itching to teach me, Sister?'

'No. I was never a teacher. But a touch of the academy wouldn't be at all unpleasant.' She looked wistful.

'Would you like me to help you catalogue the books?' I said. 'I could easily do that.'

She rounded on me, looking at me over her half-spectacles. 'Could you? Do you remember something?'

Blank. Nothing at all except the odd feeling that, once I got started I might know how to catalogue books. 'No. Nothing, I'm afraid.'

She sighed. 'Unfortunately, they're in excellent order. They're catalogued within an inch of their lives.' She stared at me. 'You're sure you don't have any feeling that you were at college? It seems to me that you're the kind of young person who goes to college as a matter of course.'

'If so, it's lost with all the rest.'

And then a week or so after, I took the ride past the horse farm, and just as I had been quite sure that I had had nothing to do with college—although I couldn't have said why—there was something about horses that seemed familiar... certainly unthreatening. Perhaps even welcoming.

Evidently Sister Bede had reported the episode to Reverend Mother Julian, because the Reverend Mother came into the office where I was transcribing, more or less accurately, some notes that she had dictated.

'I just had a thought,' she said.

I paused, white correcting fluid poised to salvage one or two typographical mistakes. 'What?'

'Why don't you go and work on a horse farm? There are several quite near. You might even be able to stay here at night, if you wanted to. There is a bus service that goes along this road. Sister Bede said you thought you knew something about horses.'

I waited for my own reaction, as I had learned to, when people had questions or suggestions as to what I might have done, or might be interested in doing. Often my reaction was unmistakably negative, though I couldn't say why, as for instance in response to Sister Martha's idea that I might get a secretarial job in the town, or Sister Ruth's that I might try being a companion to some needy elderly or sick person. But there was no such reaction this time. Instead, I suddenly saw in my mind a horse, large, gentle, chestnut, its muzzle in my hand, looking for a treat. It was a nice feeling. I put the fluid brush down. 'Yes,' I said slowly. 'I think I'd like that.'

'Sister Bede says the bus from the town runs right past several farms.'

I touched the paper with the fluid brush. 'What'll I say when they ask for experience?'

'Why don't you tell them the truth?' There

was something about the nun's steady brown eyes that made me realize that that would be the course she would take.

'But you have the courage of lions,' I told her, commenting automatically on that unspoken assumption. 'I don't.'

'You never know till you try.'

I didn't want people to know that I had lost all knowledge of who or what I was. It made me feel...disabled, crippled in some way.

The trouble with Reverend Mother Julian was that she sometimes showed an uncanny knack of picking up people's thoughts. 'If you had a gimpy leg or diabetes or something like that you'd have to tell people if it would affect what they'd demand of you or how they'd feed you.'

I didn't say anything.

'Wouldn't it be better to tell them than to let them find it out?'

'I don't want to tell them unless I have to.'

'It's your choice.'

I decided not to start with the Stanton Farm. A look through our local weekly paper, which was filled with ads offering boarding facilities and instruction at various horse farms in the area, indicated that there were several much nearer to the convent than Stanton Farm. I wanted to start earning some money so I could contribute something towards my upkeep and repay the money spent on my clothes. But I also didn't want to get too far away.

Having marked down a few farms on a map, I asked Sister Bede if I could drive the jeep.

'Can you?' she asked.

I had never even thought of the question before. 'I don't know,' I said firmly. 'But I think so.'

It turned out I could. With Sister Bede watching I stepped into the jeep, inserted the ignition key and without my conscious guidance, my hands and feet did the right things.

'I drive!' I said, feeling triumphant, after having wheeled the car around the drive.

'Wonderful!' Sister Bede said, but for safety's sake drove with me the first morning to make sure I knew what I was doing.

At the end of two discouraging days I knew that there was something to Reverend Mother Julian's suggestions about telling the truth. It made things easier. On the other hand, there was also quite a lot to my own view that in other people's eyes, loss of memory ranked in the general area of mental illness.

'What have you been doing lately?'

'I've just come out of a psychiatric institution.'

'Sorry, but we're full.'

It was an imaginary scene, of course, but it

21

kept on playing in my head in rather an alarming fashion. I went, in all, to seven places, two of them quite distant from the convent, but since I was already halfway there, I went anyway. Three of the places said, 'We've got all the help we can use, thanks.' One of the women who said that smiled and added, 'You must know that every teenage girl in the state wants to work on a horse farm—or so it seems—and most of them will gladly work for nothing but their horse's board and lessons.'

One owner said, 'What experience do you have?'

'I've worked with horses,' I replied lamely. I knew this would happen, I told myself. Why on earth hadn't I prepared something?

'Where?'

'In California,' I said desperately.

'Oh? I used to work there. Who'd you work with?'

'The Smiths,' I said, and remembered, too late, that I had given my name as Perdita Smith.

'Your family?'

'No.' I made myself smile, but my mouth was dry and my heart pounding. 'There are a lot of us Smiths.'

'So I'm told.'

At some point, I realized, he had stopped

believing me, and was looking at me in an odd fashion.

It was at the seventh place that, tired, I said baldly, 'I don't know who I am or any details of my past life, previous to the last seven months. I've lost my memory. But I just feel sure that I have worked with horses and could do so again.'

This man's expression was neither kind nor unkind, but his gaze was penetrating. Finally he said, 'I think that's a bit too much for us to handle. I'm sorry you're in that dilemma, but this is a busy farm, we board a lot of show horses, and I have to be sure that the people who work here are solid and dependable. Good luck!' And he went back inside the house.

At that point I returned to the convent.

'How was it?' Sister Bede asked, as I parked the jeep. She was collecting lettuce from the convent garden.

I sat there almost unable to talk with fatigue. I also felt terribly down. 'Awful,' I said. 'Apparently every adolescent female in the country wants to work on a horse farm, and the one time I followed Reverend Mother's advice about telling the truth and shaming the devil, the man seemed to think it was like coming out of the psycho ward. "Couldn't handle it," he said.'

'Reverend Mother's English,' Sister Bede said, as though that explained everything.

I crawled off to my bed and went to sleep, too exhausted to care whether I had dinner or not.

It was then I had a strange and frightening dream. I dreamed I was in a vividly green field. Above me was a black horse. I was down on the ground and the horse was rearing over me. Yet it wasn't the horse that frightened me. It was whoever was riding the horse. But because the horse was on its hind legs, its head up, I couldn't see the rider and had no idea who it was. All I knew was that the rider was trying to kill me. As the hooves plunged down I screamed in my dream, and found I was being shaken.

'Perdita—what's the matter?'

'He's going to kill me,' I said, still in the grip of the dream. Above me in the half-light was something black—and then I saw that it was Mother Julian's habit.

'Oh...' I let out a sigh.

Reverend Mother leaned over and pushed the switch of the light. The room sprang into complete view.

'Who was going to kill you?' Mother Julian said.

'Not the horse. The rider.'

24

'Perhaps it's not a good idea for you to work on a horse farm. I've heard about an opening—just for a clerical worker—at the town library.'

'No. The horse farm is fine. I know it won't hurt me. And I don't want to work in a library.'

'All right. Well, rest tomorrow, and then we'll see. I've brought you some dinner. You missed it downstairs in the refrectory.'

'I'm not hungry. I just want to go back to sleep.' I was still shaking a little from the dream.

'It's only a chicken sandwich and some milk. I'm sure you can manage that.'

And I could. After the first bite I realized I was ravenous. 'Thank you,' I mumbled, around the large bite of chicken and delicious home-baked bread.

Reverend Mother smiled. 'In case that's one of the things you've forgotten—you shouldn't talk with your mouth full.'

I slept a solid twelve hours. But I awoke feeling refreshed and ready to tackle the problem again. Armed with the names of four more farms, including Stanton, I set off.

The woman who said that every adolescent girl in the country wanted to work on a horse farm was not exaggerating. 'You should have come earlier in the year, before school was out' and 'We have more help than we really need,' and 'Sorry, full up,' were the comments—or variations of them—that I received at the first three farms. By the time I was ready to tackle Stanton Farm I was tired and depressed. It was, possibly for this reason, that my attention to the road was not all it should have been. I took the jeep around a curve faster than I should have, saw something looming up in front of me, wrenched the wheel, heard a screech of tyres that didn't seem to come from the jeep, and finally came to rest on some grass beside the road.

It was a shock, and I was still sitting there, taking it in and trying to catch my breath, when a voice rapped out at me from the window, 'What the hell do you think you're doing?'

I turned. An extremely angry face was glaring at me from the passenger window. I got an impression of dark hair, sunburned skin and blazing light-grey eyes.

Then the face was abruptly withdrawn and its owner, a young man in jeans and tan shirt, strode back to the trailer behind his car. It was, I saw then, a horse trailer. Opening the back, he went in. I could hear squealing and nickering and the sound of hooves thumping around.

Oh God! I thought. Did I bump into that?

26

I didn't think so. But everything happened so fast and had telescoped to such a muddle in my head I couldn't be sure.

Slowly I got out of the jeep and stood for a few seconds, feeling my legs shaking beneath me. I was reminded abruptly of my not-too-distant accident. Perhaps I hadn't recovered as much as I thought I had, I pondered, aware of a desire to get back into the jeep and return to the haven of the convent as rapidly as possible. I was saved from this, willy-nilly, by the angry young man. Backing out of the trailer he strode toward me and said, 'I want you to see what you almost did.'

Before I knew what was happening, he had a fierce grip on my arm and was dragging me over to the trailer.

'What are you doing?' I yelled.

'I'm going to try to instill some responsibility into your addled head. Look in there,' and he gave me a shove up into the trailer.

I found myself in a small, enclosed area with two other beings, one as frightened as I—a foal that surely couldn't be more than a few weeks old. Atop spindly legs, it was whiffling and nickering in a manner that showed its alarm, and the mare, its mother, was regarding me with anything but affection.

'If that foal had fallen,' the infuriated voice

said behind me, 'it could have been trampled. People like you with no sense of responsibility driving on country roads should be shot.'

From feeling frightened myself and extremely guilty, his attack had the opposite effect from the one he planned. I became almost as enraged as he.

Climbing out I said, 'I did not hit you deliberately—that is if I did hit you. And you came around that curve far too rapidly, considering you were trailing a mare and her foal. Don't you know how to pull a horse trailer? Whoever owns your stable will be mad as a hornet when he hears about the way you drive.'

Where the words came from I had no idea. They seemed to fall from some unknown slot in my head right into my mouth and get shot off my tongue. Suddenly, and with a great sense of release, I realized I had not been truly angry since I had waked up in the sanatorium, and the effect was enormously invigorating. I was sorry about any damage I had done to the horses—especially the foal—but I was reassured to see that I could stick up for myself.

The man and I glared at each other for a moment. He was very young, a boy really, not much older than me. Yet there was something about him that made the word *boy* seem inapplicable. Whatever his age, he was a man, and a tired and overworked one. How did I know that? I wondered, giving him angry stare for stare. I didn't know. But I was sure it was true.

Finally he said, 'You're right that I was driving too fast. I was thinking about...something else. But I'm right in that you were too. And to make it worse, you came around that curve on my side of the road.'

'Yes. I did. I'm sorry.' There was a short, uncomfortable silence. 'Was the foal hurt?'

'No. Nor her mother, Mollie. No thanks to either of us.'

'She's old to have this foal, isn't she?' Now where did that come from? I wondered.

'Yes, she is. And she almost died. That's another reason why...Well, she's okay. But for Pete's sake, watch where you drive.' And he stalked off to his car.

'And the same to you,' I yelled after him. Surly creep, I thought, sliding my jeep back onto the road and watching the trailer disappear through my rearview mirror. But she was a pretty mare, and the foal was a spindly-legged treasure. I devoutly hoped that nothing bad had happened to them.

The fields around Stanton Farm were luxuriant, but they were the only things about the establishment that were. The house, a frame

29

farmhouse that had been added to several times, had a run-down look, as did the barn complex to the left of the house. I looked through the courtyard gate to see if I could see any horses, but there were none in evidence. The grass bordering the drive was long and needed cutting. Parking in front of a scarred, wooden door, I rang the bell. Since I could not hear it ringing, I had no idea whether or not it worked. After a minute or so of no response, I rang again, twice.

'All right, all right,' a voice said, as the door was opened. 'I heard you the first time.'

This was obviously my day for surly people. The woman who stood facing me was good looking—very good looking. Dressed in jeans and a shirt, she was tall and slender with dark hair and eyes, and would have been a striking beauty, if her mouth were less narrow and tight and her expression less formidable.

'Yes?' she said. The word sounded more unwelcoming than I could ever remember hearing it, though, of course, I had to acknowledge that my seven months of memory wasn't that much of a test. It had the effect of driving from my unreliable head the entire little speech I had rehearsed.

'I'm looking for a job,' I blurted out.
'Doing what?'

'Taking care of horses.'

'We can't afford what is generally called a living wage.'

'How much could you afford?' At least, I thought, it was the first place that hadn't turned me down immediately.

She looked at me for a moment. Then, 'Your room and board plus seventy-five dollars a week.'

I might not remember much, I thought. But I knew beyond doubt that she was right—this was not a living wage. Still—it was my last resort. And, since I didn't want to live in, then perhaps they could afford to give me more.

'I'd rather live...at home. So you wouldn't have to board and feed me. Maybe you could up the wage?'

'No. You have to live here to be on call when we need you. You can go home every third weekend, if you want, and you can have one day off a week—that's all. I told you, the whole thing doesn't amount to more than what people think of as slave wages or conditions. Take it or leave it. After all...'

I waited for her to go on, as she obviously waited for me to tell her how I was going to respond to her invitation to take it or leave it. 'Yes?' I said, hoping she'd finish. Quite suddenly I felt tired again and discouraged. One

31

more negative statement and I'd feel free to tell her that she could keep her job—or so I thought.

'My stepson tells me that I shouldn't hire anybody at all. We can't afford it. So he'll raise hell at my offering you even what I have. But I can't help in the stables and exercise the horses and be expected to feed six or eight people seven days a week. So—do you want the job?'

'Yes,' I said, to my own great shock.

'All right. How soon can you pick up your things and get back here?

'Tomorrow?'

'I'll expect you then. Before lunch. By the way—what's your name?'

'Perdita. Perdita Smith.'

'Know anything about horses? I assumed you did since you were looking for a job. Kids your age are like locusts around here during the summer.'

'Yes,' I said, devoutly hoping she wouldn't ask me how much I knew.

'Ever taken care of them?'

'Yes.' I could feel myself beginning to blush. Evidently I was not a natural-born liar.

'Well,' she said dryly. 'You can always take over some of the kitchen if you don't know how to work in a barn. See you tomorrow.' She was about to go in when she said, 'I suppose you're on vacation from college. Which one?'

'St Hilda's.'

'Never heard of it.' Not surprising, I thought grimly, since I'd just made it up.

'It's in Canada.'

'You Canadian?'

'No. But I have relatives up there.'

'Why are you blushing?'

Unwittingly, I was sure, she was doing me a favour by the sharpness of her tone. I stopped feeling guilty and defensive and started resenting her attitude. 'I always blush when people ask me personal questions.'

Another cold stare exchanged.

'Very well,' she said. 'Please be here tomorrow as early as possible.' And she shut the door.

Working with her was not going to be a pleasure. On the other hand and perversely, I felt less depressed than if I was walking into a wonderful job with friendly people, all of whom I would have to lie to, and keep lying to with every question they asked.

CHAPTER TWO

A little to my surprise, Reverend Mother made no objection to my living at Stanton Farm. 'Some horse farms insist on that,' she said.

'But you didn't say so when I said I was going to try for a job there.'

'I didn't think about it at the time. But later it seemed obvious. An awful lot of work is done shortly after day-light.'

'You sound as though you'd worked in a barn.'

'I did, years—decades—ago.' She smiled. 'Another lifetime.'

'In England?'

'Yes. We had horses at home. When I was six, I was given my first pony. That was what I most hated giving up when I came into the order.'

'Then why—?'

'Ah, that's another story. But it has nothing to do with horses or horse farms.' She looked at me shrewdly for a moment. 'Are you trying to back out?'

34

'That woman wasn't very nice,' I muttered. Mother Julian said nothing. Then I found myself thinking about the foal and the mare in the trailer. 'But I like horses. And it isn't as though I had a huge choice.'

'You have more choice than you think you do.'

Mother Julian had a way of making me face things that I didn't want to look at. 'I suppose so,' I said shortly.

The next day I put on my jeans, put my things into a zip bag, and caught the bus to Stanton Farm.

'Remember,' Reverend Mother said, as I walked out the front door, 'you're welcome here any time, any hour. If you run into any kind of...of difficulty, just phone, and Sister Bede will come in the jeep to pick you up, or to meet you at the bus stop.'

'I thought you wanted me to go out in the world—to stop hiding,' I said grumpily.

'I did. There's a vast difference between a home you're welcome in, and a cave to hide in.' Mother Julian sounded more British than ever, which, I was beginning to realize, meant she was sternly repressing any faint sign of sentimentality.

'Good luck. God bless!' she called after me, as I stomped down the drive.

It was hot, waiting for the bus, standing on the side of the road with fields stretched out on the gently rolling hills curving up all around. The July sun beat down, even at ten in the morning. There was no shade. Further back in the fields and to the side, great trees threw their cover over large shadowed patches, but none was anywhere near me or the bus stop, and from experience I knew that if I took shelter under any of them, the bus would sweep past before I had a chance to come out and signal it. My mouth felt dried up. I was extremely thirsty. Off to one side was a pond, still, like a sheet of glass, with the white sun bouncing off of it. And then, as though it were a movie, I saw a huge black horse riding out of the white glare. On its back was a rider, but, just as in my dream, I could not see who the rider was. The horse was coming toward me and beginning to rear—but in slow motion.

It was strange, as though there were two people inside me. One believed that what I was watching was real, and wanted more than anything else to escape, to run back down the road and up the convent drive. The other knew it was a trick my mind was playing. Then, everything retreated before the overriding fact that I knew I was going to be extremely and immediately sick, and was, right there on the side of the road. When I straightened, the bus had arrived and stopped and the elderly, kind-looking driver was patting my shoulder. 'There,' he said. 'That's better. Are you all right?'

'Yes.' I glanced up. People were staring out the windows of the bus. A stout woman with a nice face got off. 'Are you sure you're all right now?' she said, as I started to move towards the bus. 'Do you live around here? Maybe you shouldn't travel today.'

'I'll be fine.' I wanted to go back to my small room in the convent. But the thought of Reverend Mother being British and stoic about my turning tail was worse than going on. I got on the bus and waited for the driver. 'Stanton Farm,' I said, when he had slid into his seat and shut the door.

He gave me my change. 'Take it easy,' he said. He still looked kind, but he also had a worried expression, as though he was afraid I might be overcome again on his clean bus.

The headache followed, of course, and the jouncing of the bus did nothing to help. Always before I had retreated to my room and lain down. Now there was no retreat. As the invisible talons seemed to close in over my forehead, I shut my eyes and, for the next half hour, took slow, deep breaths. Somewhat to my surprise, the claws retracted, the pain and giddiness retreated. I still had a headache, but it was bearable. I opened my eyes. There were still fields of wheat and other grain, but more hilly pasture land, criss-crossed by fences and stone walls. The trees marched nearer to the road, breaking here and there to admit a view of a country house, or farm house. Horses grazed. Barns loomed bigger than the homes next to them. There was another burst of trees, then more open land with hills at the back, and a post appeared, with a sign blowing slightly in the breeze. I could see, right away, why I hadn't noticed it before. New, the black letters on a white background, with a silhouette of a horse underneath, would have been highly visible. But the black was scratched and the white was grey and smeared. I remembered then the house, and the somewhat abandoned look of the grass around it, and the window trim that need fresh paint.

'Stanton Farm,' the bus driver called out, and the bus pulled to the side.

My legs felt shaky, and I could feel anxiety washing over me. I watched the bus drive off, and then stood there, looking down the drive.

It was a pleasant house, I decided, of no particular shape, as though it had started out

38

as a medium-sized farm house and had been added to in a haphazard fashion, with one extension going off to the right, and on the left what looked like the end of another addition going back at right angles to the main part. Like houses in England...*and how did I know that?'*

I stood there, gripping the shoulder strap of my zip bag, and saw, as though in another dimension, on a screen in my mind, another house, a stone house bigger and more prosperous looking, less a farmhouse, more a...a manor house...

Finding I was standing next to the post, I leaned against it. I could feel the moisture on my forehead, and put up a hand to wipe it off.

It wasn't a dream, or some kind of vision or hallucination; it was memory. What was it one of the many doctors had said?—'It will come back, possibly in bits and pieces...'

It wasn't a large piece, and it still had a dreamlike quality. Yet I knew it was real. I knew I had been there, though I didn't know for how long or why. But behind the English house, behind the trees, I could see the hills rising, to the great bald green moors, with stone walls climbing over them, and horses climbing up, horses with riders...

I don't know how long I would have stood

there, leaning against the post, staring down the dirt and gravel drive to the house and stables thirty yards away. But the woman who had hired me came out of the barn into the courtyard beside the left extension of the house, leading a horse, which she tied to the side of the barn by attaching the lead shank to a ring in the wall. Then she started brushing the horse.

Walking down the drive, I opened the gate to the courtyard and came in. The horse, a big chestnut, turned and looked at me, its ears flat. A nervous and difficult animal, I found myself thinking, looking at its points. There was Thoroughbred there, and also something else—perhaps quarter horse. The gelding had a big-boned and well-muscled body and appeared as though it would be good for hunting. I walked around the horse, giving its hindquarters plenty of room, and found the woman on the other side brushing the horse with a round curry-comb. She glanced up at me. 'Oh, it's you. What did you say your name was? Perdita Smith? Well, Perdita, I might as well see now what you can do. Go in and get a horse named Bayou. You'll find him on the left as you go in the barn. His owner is coming in half an hour. Bring him out here and get him ready. The tack is hanging on the wall over his nameplate, and you'll see boxes with grooming gear around the equipment room. You can put your bag down inside, I'll show you your room later.'

'All right...er—I'm afraid I don't know your name.'

She straightened. Her brows rose. 'I thought surely you must have known before you showed up here. I'm Penelope Stanton.'

'Oh.' I was dismayed by the thought that she might be a member of the Stanton family and—most probably—the owner. 'You own the farm, Mrs Stanton?'

'No. I thought I made that clear. My stepson does. He's in the ring now, instructing. Obviously you don't come from around here. I should have thought you'd find out about such things before you applied for a job. And you'd better call me Penelope,' she finished grudgingly, 'everyone else does.'

'I'll get the horse,' I said, and beat a rapid retreat. My heart was thumping uncomfortably, and my headache, which had seemed to settle somewhat, started to throb again. I walked through the big barn door into a square space where another horse, a smaller, chunkier brown horse was being readied by an elderly groom. His thick, coarsened hands were touching the horse delicately here and there, running over various parts of the skin, and then either

41

touching them with a brush or rubbing them slightly with a rag. Quietly, as he worked, he kept up a low murmur to the horse. Then he caught sight of me and the murmur stopped. 'Yes?' he said.

'I'm Perdita Smith. I'm the new barn help.'

'John didn't tell me he was hiring again.' He sounded suspicious, even hostile.

'I was hired by Penelope Stanton.'

The horse had turned around to look at me, then stamped its back foot, moving around. 'Whoa there,' he said. 'No need to get upset.' The gnarled hands moved over the nose and neck. 'She never told me,' he grumbled.

'I'm supposed to get Bayou.'

'You'd better get him then, hadn't you?'

There was something about his voice, or his speech, that struck a cord in me somewhere, I thought, going to the left as Penelope had told me. Entering a wing of the barn with stalls on both sides of an aisle, I passed a grooming stall to the left, two empty stalls opposite, and finally arrived at a stall with a card bearing the name BAYOU inserted into a slot on the post. The stall contained a medium-sized roan horse, peering at me through the linked gate. I picked up a grooming halter hanging outside the gate and then slipped in. Rubbing the horse on his long face and neck, I slipped the halter on and led him out, past the brown horse and into the courtyard, tying him to the ring on the wall opposite to where Penelope was grooming the big chestnut. There were several rings on both walls, and without thinking I chose one as far from the chestnut as possible. Then I went back, found a box with grooming equipment, returned and went to work.

I was right about one thing, I found out. I liked horses and felt comfortable around them. Just as in the case of driving the jeep, my hands seemed to act from a memory of their own. Bayou was plainly no aristocrat, but he was a pleasant horse, nicely put together, about fifteen hands, with an attractive personality. I brushed and rubbed and talked to him, inspecting his feet and his belly. And he seemed to respond, lowering his head once or twice and nuzzling my shoulder.

Since I'd waked up in the convent, I reflected, I'd not felt this much at ease. My mind went back to the memory of the stone house in England. It was not completely clear, and though I could see and remember people moving around, I could not see their faces or recall their names. It was as though it had happened a long time ago. But it was different from a dream or a hallucination of some kind. I felt strongly that it was an ordinary memory, perhaps from

43

early childhood, and I also felt that it was a pleasant memory.

I worked and brushed and rubbed and talked to the horse in a quiet voice. 'You have a pretty face,' I said very quietly, 'although I wouldn't expect you to come from some highfalutin family. I wonder who owns you and whether they treat you well...' Why, I wondered, had that question come into my mind at all?

'We don't have time for playing with the horses,' Penelope's sharp voice said behind me.

I leaned over and unhooked the tack I'd brought out and hung on the barn wall. Then I picked up some saddle soap and a wet sponge and went to work. My first instinct was to answer in kind. But something held me back. Perhaps, I thought, it was the realization that this was Penelope's usual manner and unless I wanted to live in continued hostility, I'd better reserve my fire for times when I needed it. 'When does the owner arrive?'

'She's here now. Come on, Nancy?'

I turned and saw a tall, thin child of about thirteen coming out of the barn in a hunting cap, breeches and boots. Pale hair was gathered in a pony tail, and light brown eyes peered at the horse.

'Nancy, darling, this is Perdita, our new barn

helper.' Penelope glanced at me. 'This is my daughter, Nancy Schwartz. She's a great little horsewoman.' Her voice sharpened. 'Please take Bayou over to the mounting block over there so Nancy can get on.'

'I don't feel very well,' Nancy said.

'Yes you do, darling. You felt perfectly well an hour ago.' She glanced at the child. 'Now you know you're a good rider, and you'll soon be an even better one, and start winning prizes at all the shows.' She addressed me again. 'Nancy's been praised for her seat by some of the best. Now help her mount.'

I led Bayou over to the mounting block and turned him so that Nancy could get up on the right side. Bayou, I noticed, who had stood quite still while I groomed him, was shifting around a little.

'Whoa, Bayou, take it easy,' I said. 'Be still now.' I kept my hand on the reins close to the snaffle while Nancy climbed up on the mounting block.'

Nancy put her left foot in the stirrup, clutched the back of the saddle with her right hand, drew herself up and, releasing the saddle, swung her other leg over.

'Adjust your rein,' I said automatically.

Penelope came up on the other side, lifted the reins from Bayou's neck, and when Nancy had settled herself, handed the reins to her. 'Always remember to hold the reins in your left hand when you mount and then take them in both hands when you sink into the saddle. You must be nervous with a new person helping you, otherwise you'd remember that.'

'All right,' Nancy said compliantly.

Surely, I thought, Penelope's not going to send this child out alone. She couldn't be more than thirteen. As though in answer to my un-asked question, there was the sound of hooves coming through the doorway on the opposite side of the courtyard, the side across from where I had come in. At that moment a group of young people on horseback came through, followed by a young man. With a jolt, I saw beneath the black visor the features of the man in the van whose horse trailer I had pushed off the road. He was busy talking to the four young women who were dismounting.

'All right, then, Sally, you'll be here Tuesday, Mary, you're coming in for an extra hour Monday, Jane and Kitty, I'll see you the same time next week.'

I was standing there, frozen. Well, I thought, there went the job. Expecting a sense of relief, I was a little surprised to feel, instead, ap-prehension. Why on earth would I want to keep a job at less than a living wage in a run-down-looking stable, under the supervision of a hostile woman and in the employ of a surly boss? Nevertheless, and inconsistently, I found myself sorry that I was about to lose it. Because John Stanton, who had finally noticed me, was glaring at me with gathering rage.

'What are you doing here?'

'Mrs Stanton hired me.'

He swung toward her. 'Penelope—what on earth...' Everyone had stopped talking and started watching.

'John,' she said, her voice as cold as iron, 'this is Perdita Smith. She was hired to help me out in both the barn and the kitchen. And—as I'm sure you know—I can use help.'

There was a long, strained silence. Then John said, 'Just for your information, this girl, whatever her name is, nearly ran down Mollie and her foal in the trailer when I was taking them to the clinic.'

She turned to me. 'Is this true?'

'Yes,' I said. Why bother to lie? 'And it's also true that he came around the corner much too fast.'

'Well, John? Remember, I've seen your driving sometimes.'

He hesitated. 'My driving isn't perfect. It's true I was coming too fast around that bridge corner. I was partly at fault.' He took his

47

hunting cap off, wiped his forehead against his arm, and glanced at me. 'But maybe I'm surprised you didn't ask me first.'

'I'll leave if you wish,' I said huffily.

'You'll do as I say,' Penelope said. 'John—do you want to continue this conversation out here?'

'No,' he said shortly. 'If you hired her, so be it. But keep her away from me. All right, Nancy, you can come out to the ring.'

I watched them walk the horses back through the archway. John Stanton was riding a large bay. He held it back, letting Nancy ride out ahead of him. I saw her post up and down, her knees clutching, her hands in a deathlike grip on the reins.

'Remember, darling,' her mother called after her, 'there's nothing to be afraid of.' She turned to me. 'You can start on one of the horses. Get its saddle off and sponge it down. There's a hose over there. And just by the way of general comment, you'll be too busy to stand around dreaming. You and Jeremy will be responsible for the horses. Lucian—my son—helps when he can. But he's busy most of the time now, and I have other things to do. So you'd better get started.'

'Where do I put my things?'

'Opposite Bayou's stall there's a staircase

going up to the top floor of the barn. The room on your left is Jeremy's. Yours is on the right. You share the bath. Your meals are in the kitchen of the house. Breakfast is at seven, lunch at one and dinner at seven.'

Hosing down the grey, I reflected that with no effort at all I had managed to get myself into a job where no matter what I did, someone was bound to be angry at me.

I was expecting the worst when I finally got my bag upstairs to the top section of the barn, and was therefore pleasantly surprised to find it not as bad as I expected. The little stair led up into a narrow hall between two wooden walls. To the left was one door, with the name Jeremy Walsh inserted into a little slot at eye level, and to the right another, with no name in the slot. Straight ahead, its door open, was a large bathroom. Going in, I saw on old-fashioned bathtub up on clawed feet, but polished clean, and a shower curtain that could be pulled around it. The window looked out towards the frame house. Opening the door on the right, I went into a medium-sized bedroom. The panelled wall only rose to about seven feet. Above were the rafters of the barn, and filling the air was the sweet, pungent aroma of hay. A door on the far side of the room was now closed. I went across, opened it, and found myself in the hayloft. The hay rose six feet to the left and right of me. Straight ahead was another narrow staircase going down, I suspected, to the other wing of the barn.

'You'll be having to keep the door closed, I'm thinking,' a male voice said behind me.

I turned. Jeremy was standing in my doorway, his narrow eyes glinting at me. 'There's rats in that hay.'

Hastily I shut the door. 'Thanks.'

He grunted, and started to leave.

'Penelope was grooming a big chestnut,' I said suddenly. 'A good-looking horse but sort of edgy. Is he a Stanton horse?'

'He is not,' Jeremy said promptly. 'More's the pity. He belongs to Estes Conrad, who'll be in the ring now, working the poor beast half to death.'

'Who is he?'

'His high and mightiness. That's who he is.' And Jeremy disappeared out of the room. I heard the bathroom door shut and water start running.

Lunch was at one. At ten minutes to one I followed Jeremy down a long aisle between stalls leading into the back of the house and from there we went into the kitchen. The latter was large and old fashioned, with a wooden table in the middle, covered by an oilcloth, a range stretching over all of one side, and, on another side, a gas stove and oven. Wood was piled in one small room off the kitchen, and what looked like a pantry with shelves of preserves and canned food in another. John Stanton sat at one end and Penelope the other. Nancy and I sat on one side with Jeremy opposite. She had taken off her cap, and her fine, light brown hair clung to her narrow face.

'How did the ride go, darling?' Penelope said.

'Fine.'

Penelope put an iron pot containing what looked like stew on the table in front of her and sat down. Dishes were piled at her plate and she started filling them and passing them down the table. 'What did you work on this morning?'

'Trotting and some cantering.'

'Jumping?'

'No.' I saw Nancy glance nervously at John.

Without looking up he said, 'She's not ready for that yet.'

'Nonsense. I had her jumping last week.'

'I'd rather wait, Mummy, until I feel a bit...' She glanced at John again. '...a bit more sure.'

'She has to be more secure on the horse first,

relax more. Don't push her.' John reached out and took some bread, then passed it to Nancy.

'Well if you deliberately *make* her nervous, then I can see why she would be unsure. She wasn't that way with me.'

'Was I deliberately making you nervous, Nancy?' John Stanton asked sarcastically.

My heart went out to the child. From the small amount I'd seen, she was certainly not a good rider. But if she'd been terrorized until her confidence had broken, I could see why she wasn't better.

Nancy didn't say anything, but picked at her food.

'Well?'

'Maybe she doesn't like to be yelled at,' I heard myself say, and marvelled at my own stupidity.

I saw the light grey eyes focus on me again. 'I don't think this concerns you,' John said.

'Perhaps it doesn't,' Penelope put in. 'But Perdita has a point. People—especially children—who are scolded and belittled seldom make good riders.'

'I neither scold nor scream, and you're welcome to come out to the ring and see for yourself.'

'Please...' Nancy said. One tear ran down her sallow cheek. 'May I be excused?' And before her mother could reply, she'd fled the table.

'Nancy is a good rider,' Penelope said, her nostrils looking pinched and arched. 'Estes, who should know, has said she handled a horse well. The fact that she seems...well...nervous, is directly attributable to you, John, and I won't have it. If she started showing and winning a prize or two, we'd attract more pupils, and we might be able to do something with this place.'

John pushed his empty plate away towards the salad bowl and helped himself. 'This conversation, in front of Jeremy and...and Miss Smith...is highly inappropriate. You and I disagree how to bring this place back. If we want to continue the discussion, let's do it in private.'

Penelope didn't reply. After a minute she looked at me. 'More stew, Perdita?'

'No thanks.' The stew had been, I felt reasonably sure, left over from leftovers. *Leftovers*, I thought. The word just dropped into my mind, I could not remember hearing it. But I knew what it meant, just the way I knew what John and Penelope were talking about, although I wasn't able to figure out Nancy's particular problem—other than being taught by her arbitrary and tyrannical stepbrother.

'When's Conrad coming back?' John asked suddenly, helping himself to a chunk of the French bread.

'Who knows?' Jeremy grumbled.

'Estes Conrad pays handsomely to have that horse stabled here, and he's one of the best riders in this part of the country,' Penelope Stanton said. 'We're lucky he's stuck with us, instead of going to Lambert Farm or the Devereux stables as so many others have done.'

'Estes rides with Devereux,' John said. 'He has another horse there.'

'Yes, I know,' Penelope agreed sharply. 'But he's loyal to Stanton. And for that we should be grateful.'

Lambert and Devereux. Those were two of the stables I'd gone to—big places, with several grooms and instructors and all the appurtenances that indicated an expensively and well-run barn.

'We're grateful,' John said, irony evident in his voice.

'And well you might be.' Penelope got up. 'Perdita, we have some more people coming in at two. I want Jessup, Rosebud, Randy and Graymalkin got ready and saddled.'

'Not Graymalkin,' John said. He polished off the salad dressing on his plate with a piece of bread. 'Any coffee?'

'It'll be ready in a minute. Why not Gray-malkin?'

'I don't want him ridden by Robin Oates—and you usually give him to her.'

'John—she asked for him. She's thinking of buying him.'

'He's not for sale—certainly not to her.'

'Ach, don't be foolish!' Jeremy said. 'Don't be your father's son.'

'And don't speak to me like that.'

Jeremy looked at him for a moment. Then arose from his chair and walked out.

'I'm told,' Penelope said, taking the coffee-pot from the stove, 'that Jeremy put you on your first pony when you were four years old. Do you have to talk to him like that?'

John got up abruptly and went to the door.

'I thought you wanted coffee,' Penelope said.

'I changed my mind,' her stepson replied over his shoulder, going out.

I was cleaning tack in the yard after lunch when there was the sound of hooves coming into the courtyard. In a few seconds the big chestnut came through the gate. It was breathing heavily and its sides and neck were dark with sweat and stained with lather. The rider, who swung himself off, had thick fair hair that shone in the sun. Under the rolled up sleeves, his arms were tanned and muscled. He looked somewhere in his thirties.

'Hey, Jeremy!' he called towards the old groom who was coming into the yard. 'This horse should have more oats. He almost fell asleep on his feet. I had to use the crop several times, and he balked at at least two of the fences.'

'You're a lazy beast,' Jeremy said, removing the saddle and bridle and putting on a grooming halter. 'Now come along and I'll cool you off. No, no you don't. Not yet. You're too hot. You can have some water later when you've cooled down.'

'You're new around here, aren't you?'

I looked up. Piercing blue eyes seemed to smile at me out of a tanned face. Estes Conrad, I thought with a jolt, was probably one of the most attractive men I'd ever seen in my life.

'Contrary to what you're thinking,' he said. 'I did not ride that brute too hard. For one thing he sweats easily, and for another he wastes a lot of energy and effort in balking at almost every fence. What's your name?'

'Perdita Smith.' I could feel myself blushing.

'Well, Perdita, you're a welcome addition to the stables. Where do you come from?'

It was such an innocent question. But it threw me into a panic. I could feel myself getting red. My mind was blank. I couldn't even invent something.

'Or is it a case of "Where did you come from baby dear, The blue skies opened and I am here"?'

I laughed, and the jammed computer in my mind loosened. *Jammed computer*, I thought. Where did I get that? My tongue seemed to act out of its own brain.

'England,' I said. I thought again of the manor house.

'Yes, I was going to guess that. You have a slight English accent.'

Did I? If so, no one had commented on it before, which was odd considering I had spent hours with doctors and psychologists as they probed and questioned about one region of the country after another to see if any one sounded familiar. *Does this scene jog any memory, Perdita? No? Then let's try this...* ' And on and on the photographs would go, motion pictures sometimes. There were strange flashes sometimes, or feelings as I looked at certain scenes. And when that happened, the photographs were put in front of me again, or different scenes of the same area, to see if the reaction would persist. But it never had. How strange that no one had said, 'You have a slight English accent. Let's try for some English scenery.'

57

'Have I said something wrong?' The voice beside and a little above me sounded concerned.

'Sorry, no. I was...wool gathering.'

'Where in England?'

'Yorkshire.'

'Oh—what part?'

'In the country outside York.' As I said it, I knew it was true. But who was I there with? And it was long ago.

'Did you ride much?'

'Of course.'

He smiled. 'Probably had your own pony.'

'Yes—Jingle.'

And then I saw myself, an earnest, square-faced nine-year-old, with my father.

'Now take Jingle slowly. He's not too young and he has his dignity to consider. When you get used to him he'll be easier to trot and canter.' The scene washed over me like a breaker.

'I'm so sorry, what on earth have I said? Here, for heaven's sake!'

It was only when I saw the handkerchief thrust at me, that I realized tears were pouring down my cheeks. His brows drawn together in concern, Estes Conrad was watching me.

'I'm sorry,' I said. 'It's just...' How could I explain that I was not only crying over my lost father, who, I knew now, was dead, and had been dead for a long time, but because of the fact that I remembered at all....

'Estes, how are you? Perdita, what in heaven's name is the matter?' Penelope, in riding breeches and boots, had come over.

'I think I've said something that upset her,' Estes said. 'I'm so sorry!'

'Well you really must pull yourself together, Perdita. I'm sure whatever it was wasn't meant, and you really can't be that sensitive.'

I managed to get myself under control. 'It's not that.' I looked straight at Estes. 'You didn't say anything. I mean—I was remembering my father, who died.'

'I see. Clumsy of me.'

'No.' I put in, before Penelope could speak. 'Not at all.' And I walked off with the tack into the tack room before anything more could be said.

It was queer, I thought, hanging the bridles over the hooks from which I'd taken them, I was more shaken by the return of a chunk of memory than I had been by having none at all. It was true that I had now acquired a past, or at least a segment of past, which I had not had. But I could also see that there was a certain peace in no past whatsoever. To see one part and one person clearly but nothing else and no other person somehow emphasized my curious

59

mental state. I felt more of a cripple than I had before.... I also felt shaken. I stood there for a moment, my hand on the hook, seeing my father clearly. He, too, was blond and blue-eyed, though not as tall as Estes, and somehow stockier. Neither was he handsome, yet he had the kindest face I had ever known. I realized now that I knew that he was killed in a car accident when I was away from home, so that when I had said goodbye to him before going to school, that time was the last time I had seen him. Then I started remembering school...the building, the uniforms we wore.... But I could not remember my mother; nor, strangest of all, could I remember my name. Although at moments such as when I recalled my father talking to me, I knew he addressed me by name, but the name itself strayed just beyond reach.

'Perdita—'

I turned. Penelope was coming into the tack room, putting down the tack box with its grooming equipment and the name of the horse, Ransom, painted on the front. 'Are you all right?'

'Yes, fine. I'm sorry about what happened. It's just...I can't...' *How on earth could I explain?* 'It was terribly stupid—and nothing he really meant, just something he said reminded me of my father—and as a matter of fact, he looks like him, sort of.'

Her face, which had been pulled tight, relaxed a little. 'I see. Well, all right. But do get yourself pulled together. I hired you over John's dead body, so to speak, as I'm sure you know. And if you don't pull your weight, or succumb to fits of temperament, he will have just cause to insist you go.'

'Yes, all right. It won't happen again.'

That night I fell asleep, exhausted. By the end of the day I'd mucked out my regular dozen stalls plus two extra that had somehow been missed, groomed nine horses and cleaned assorted tack,and I was unused to what amounted to hard, physical labour.

'I hope you know how to ride,' Penelope had said just before I dragged myself upstairs from the supper table. 'Because I want you to exercise some of the horses tomorrow. Some are ours, and others are boarders whose owners haven't been in for a while, and they need some exercise and schooling. Just turning them out isn't enough—especially if we're supposed to show them.'

'Fine,' I made myself say. John Stanton was there, half-working on some accounts while he ate his dinner.

'Which horses?' he asked, without looking up.

'Rosebud, Graymalkin, and Mouse.'

'Umm,' he said. And then, 'All right.' I had the curious feeling that he was going to object, but changed his mind at the last moment.

I fell asleep in the narrow cot within a moment of hitting the pillow. And then, at some point later, woke up, with the feeling that I'd had vivid and unsettling dreams, though I couldn't remember what they were.

I glanced at the clock beside my bed. Two o'clock. Pale moonlight poured through the big barn window, although all I could see from my bed were stars. Over the high room dividers came the smell of hay, and the sound of Jeremy's not-so-gentle snores. From below I could hear the occasional stamping of hooves and nicker of horses. Then, between snores, I thought I heard something else, drowned out, each time Jeremy took in a long, high, audible breath, and after a pause, let it out again. I strained my ears. Yes, there, in a moment of silence, it was, a faint mewing. I got up and peered out the window. It was a huge opening, intended as a chute for the hay, so the sill only came to an inch or so above my knees. The courtyard below seemed infinitely peaceful, with the occasional horse smell or horse sound drifting up from below, but the mewing had disappeared. Either it had stopped, or I was listening in the wrong place. Stepping back, I went into the middle of the room and paused. No, it hadn't disappeared. There, between snores, it was, coming from...I turned myself slowly round, and finally decided that the point of origin was the other side of the door leading to the hayloft. Taking one step I paused for a moment. Jeremy had warned me about the rats in the hayloft. I loved animals, and recognized that rats had their place in the cosmic scheme of things, but I preferred to respect rats at a distance and not in my bedroom. But one more mew, sounding somehow more urgent than the others made me go over and open the door a fraction. A small dark shape slid in. 'I just hope you're a cat, and not something else,' I whispered as I closed the door. I received another mew in reply, and felt the soft fur brush against my leg.

I got back into bed, and felt a light plop immediately afterwards. Then the cat—or kitten—marched up the bed, and put its face down to mine. Thoughts about country cats and fleas went vividly through my mind, adding to my store of interesting things I seemed to remember. Then I put a hand up to stroke the cat and saw her silhouette shrink back.

'Sorry, kitty,' I said. Obviously, not all her life had been happy, nor all her experience of people. The image of John Stanton's unyielding face slid across my mind. I could well imagine him disciplining a kitten who got in his way or in the way of one of his horses. Indignation filled me. By this time the cat had burrowed its way into the space between my shoulder and neck and had turned itself round and round and then sat down. I waited awhile, then slowly, very slowly, put up a hand and rubbed the back next to my neck. A loud rumbling purr broke out, and the more I stroked the noisier the purrs became until they seemed on the verge of rivaling Jeremy's efforts in the next room.

'Shh,' I said. 'You'll wake up the landscape.' The cat purred louder than ever. By this time, something told me that my bedmate was indeed still a kitten. There was a fragility of the bones in the skinny body that indicated extreme youth.

'Good night,' I said drowsily, and, to the sound of purrs, dropped into a sleep that this time proved dreamless.

CHAPTER THREE

The next day, after cleaning out about ten stalls, I groomed and saddled Rosebud, a brown horse of no particular ancestry, and rode her out into the trails behind the farm. I knew that I had not ridden for at least six months, and for all I could remember, it might have been much longer than that. I could feel my unused muscles protesting mildly as Rosebud broke from a walk into a trot, and then a canter. But sore muscles or not, it was a delight. My hands, my legs and the rest of my body responded with an intelligence and intuition of their own. Rosebud was a nice horse, lively at first through lack of exercise, and certainly no problem. The trail went over some open pasture and I let her canter on. She was a good mover and pleasant, but she stopped easily the minute I let her and was certainly not top show material. Having found myself with that conclusion, as though it had been dictated into my head by someone else, I tried, consciously, to remember shows I had attended. Plainly I knew something about the world of horses and horse shows.... But the moment I tried, concentrating, the whole thing stopped working. What a weird thing the mind was! Discouraged, I allowed Rosebud to settle back to a walk.

'Come along, Rosebud!' I said aloud, after a few minutes of that. I squeezed her with my legs, and she broke into a trot. 'All right,' I said, 'let's have another canter.' And off we went. The trail, which led through some trees and around a pond of some kind, seemed clear and moderately straight—no blind turns. So I urged her into a gallop. 'Wow! That was good,' I said, pulling up at the end. 'Rosebud, you did fine!'

I trotted her for a while, circling half the reservoir, and then walked her back, passing the riding ring as I approached the stable.

It was a big ring, with a course of jumps set up and with room beyond that for flat work. John Stanton was in the ring, minus hat, his dark hair ruffled, instructing three young girls.

'Come on, Megan, let's get serious! You're not sitting straight, your heels aren't down, and you're hanging onto the reins too hard, which is bad for the horse's mouth. You look like a sack of potatoes. Lower your arms, now!'

And, with a stifled giggle, Megan obediently did.

'Now trot!'

Once Megan got herself together, she rode well, her narrow body rising easily from the saddle, her leg steady.

'Now take the jump!'

She did that fairly well, too.

'Good! Next—Nancy. Now take it easy. Pick up a trot, circle, and then take the jump.'

I hadn't noticed, until that moment, that Nancy Schwartz, Penelope's daughter, was among the girls. But the moment she started to trot her horse, I recognized the queer, jerky movements I'd seen the night before. It was obvious, from yards away, that while Megan was basically at ease on the big grey she was riding, Nancy, on a much smaller, quieter horse, was not.

'No, you don't have to rise that much, try to feel the motion of the horse—let it push you forward and up. And don't hang onto the reins like that. Ride from your legs, not from the reins.'

As I watched, Nancy made a stab at following each of the instructions barked at her by John Stanton. She tried to rise more easily with the motion of the horse instead of shooting up in the saddle, slackened her hold on the reins, and then automatically closed her legs and heels into the horse's side. The effect was immediate and predictable. The horse broke into a trot and then a canter. Nancy forgot all about not hanging onto the reins and tugged them for dear life. 'I can't stop him!' she yelled.

'Hold the reins steadily. Don't jerk on them like that!' And then, *'Don't* hang on his mouth! It isn't made of steel. It's his most sensitive part.' The words were scarcely out before the horse flung up its head and tried to rear. By this time he and his rider had circled quite near me.

'Nancy,' I said quietly, and as evenly as I could. 'Now lower your arms a little, and sit back, straight. He'll obey better that way. Easy now. He isn't going to hurt you. Just drop your hands.'

Miraculously, she did. The horse came to a standstill, stamping and trying to free its head. John came over and took hold of the rein above the bit. 'All right?' he asked her.

Nancy, who was, I was almost certain, on the brink of tears, nodded.

Then John looked at me, and we stared at each other for a moment. Finally he said, 'I'd like to talk to you later.'

Obviously he did not like his teaching interferred with, and I was in for a dressing down. Well, I thought, too bad. I'd be happy to give as good as I got. After all, Penelope hired me, and I was reasonably convinced that she would not permit her stepson to unhire me.

'Very well,' I said. 'I'll be back at the barn.' And I clucked Rosebud to a sedate walk towards the stable. The truth was, I thought, as I got off and hosed her down, that I was not absolutely convinced that if John Stanton wanted to get rid of me he couldn't do it.

I was in the midst of brushing Mouse, a smallish, dappled grey with the short, slightly dished face that betrayed an Arab strain, when the girls from the ring rode into the courtyard, followed by John on foot.

'Lucian!' John yelled.

A good-looking blond boy of about sixteen came out of the tackroom and started to unsaddle three of the horses after the girls got off.

'Nancy,' John went on, after the other girls had left, 'you're going to groom Bayou, aren't you?'

'All right.' She had slid off the saddle, and was standing holding the pommel when Bayou turned his head round and looked at her. Nancy took a step back. The reins slid off Bayou's neck, and he started to walk towards the barn.

'Watch it,' I said, without thinking. I caught Bayou's reins, then pulled them up on his back and knotted them.

'Nancy—' John exploded.

Nancy burst into tears and ran out of the courtyard, bumping into her mother coming through the gate.

'Nancy, what happened? Have you hurt yourself?'

But Nancy veered off and went towards the house. Penelope came over, her mouth in a tight line. 'Have you been bullying her, John?'

'As a horsewoman yourself,' he said acidly, 'you're surely the first to agree that rule number one is you don't let go the reins so that the horse can trip over them and break a leg.' He took hold of Bayou and led him into the barn.

Penelope looked at me as I combed Mouse's tail and mane. 'Nancy is a very nice little rider,' she said, an angry undertone in her voice. 'She only...panics...when she feels terrorized. And John treats her as though she were some kind of idiot, which she's not. If he'd just unclench his hand and let me hire a decent instructor—but it's no use getting you involved in that.' She glanced at Mouse. 'I gather you've already been out on Rosebud and Graymalkin.'

'No, just Rosebud.'

'Well, you'll really have to get some speed on. Neither Mouse nor Graymalkin are worth much time being spent on them. Personally, if it were my farm—but it's not. John's father left it to him and that's that. Get them exercised as fast as you can. They're not the kind of horses that are going to do this place any credit, and I don't want you wasting effort on them.' And she walked off.

'Mouse,' I said, as we rode the path back to the trail, 'you have undistinguished ancestry. Does it bother you?' Mouse gave a happy little grunt and, at the slightest touch of my leg, broke first into a trot and then a canter. He might be the people's horse, I thought, but he was a delight. Unlike Rosebud, whose favourite pastime was eating while doing nothing at all, Mouse was lively and full of energy, and taking him over the same ground I came back in a lot shorter time. When I returned after taking his saddle into the tack room, I was touched when he rubbed his nose against my chest.

'Well, well,' I said, scratching him behind his ears. 'Such affection, and after such a short acquaintance.'

'He wants a carrot,' John Stanton's voice said. I turned around. He was looking at me with a certain satirical amusement. 'Here,' he said, taking a carrot out of his pocket, 'you'll make a friend for life.'

Mouse ate the carrot so fast, he almost inhaled it. Then he started nosing around my pockets for more.

'Where is the source for carrots?'

'There are some in a box in there. But hold off for a moment.' He scowled. 'I still think Penelope shouldn't have hired you, and where we're going to get your salary from I don't know.'

'Want me to leave?' I held my breath. He might call my bluff.

'Not at the moment. You seem to know what you're doing.' He glanced up at me from under his straight brows. 'As I'm sure you knew when you asked that. What's your background? Where have you worked?'

The question came at me out of the blue. I had been so preoccupied with Rosebud, Bayou and Mouse, and with Nancy's problems, that I had forgotten that I couldn't remember. And my mind went blank.

I noticed his eyebrows came down in another scowl. 'Well?'

'In England,' I said finally.

'Oh? Where?'

'Yorkshire.'

'You don't have that much of an accent—although there is some there.'

'I lived part time over here, part there.'

'Where over here?'

It was like trying to dodge a pursuer. I took a deep breath. 'Small farms you wouldn't have heard of—boarding stables, most of them. I worked during school vacations—that kind of thing.' The moment those words were out of my mouth, I knew I'd made a mistake. I should never have mentioned school.

'Where did you go to school?'

'In England,' I said promptly. Then, remembering my supposedly dual upbringing. 'And Oregon.' Why I picked that I wasn't sure, except that it sounded safely remote from the East.

'Oh? What school?'

'Chadwick.'

'Don't know it.'

'It's a newish boarding school,' I said, having just invented it.

'They ride there?'

'Sure. Lots.'

'Are you going to college?'

'I guess so.'

'Which one?'

'Haven't made up my mind yet.'

My heart was thumping in an alarming fashion. Since I'd waked up in the convent seven months before, I'd never been asked so many questions by someone who did not know about my head injury. The psychiatrists and doctors questioned me endlessly, but they were well aware of my mental blanks.

73

'You've taught, haven't you?'

That caught me off guard. 'Yes,' I said. Curious. I had no hesitation about that.

'Then maybe you can help me out with the children—the beginners. That'll leave me more time to train myself, and school a couple of people who're getting ready for shows.'

'All right. If I have time. Penelope's given me twelve horses to take care of, plus exercising four. That's not going to leave me a lot of spare hours.'

He smoothed Mouse's mane. 'I'll talk to her.'

Jeremy always took care of Ransom, Estes Conrad's big chestnut, and he was supposed to have the horse saddled and waiting when Estes parked his handsome royal blue Mercedes outside the gate and came in. When Jeremy was unavailable, Penelope readied Ransom. But two days later Jeremy was off collecting a shipment of feed, and Penelope was taking care of Nancy, who had had a virus attack, when Estes called and said he'd be coming around eleven in the morning.

'You'll have to get him ready, Perdita,' Penelope said, calling out Nancy's window. 'But for heaven's sake, be careful. He's not sweet tempered. Watch yourself!'

I could see what she meant the moment I walked up to the corner stall where Ransom lived in comparative luxury. No one had cleaned out his stall that morning, and the shavings used to cover the concrete floor were black and wet with droppings. Ransom was not pleased, whether about the state of his stall, or out of a negative view of life in general, I didn't know. When I walked up and unlatched the door to the stall he put his ears back and gave me an evil glare.

'All right, Ransom,' I said, 'this isn't going to be fun for either of us. But we might as well come to some kind of an agreement.' Ransom's ears went even flatter, and his lip raised, showing a splendid set of teeth. I could hardly tell myself that I'd never before been afraid of a horse, because I couldn't remember whether I had or hadn't. Yet, with the exception of the nightmare about the rearing black horse, I could summon no echo of more than ordinary anxiety as Ransom did everything a horse can do short of speaking the words 'Get out of my stall and leave me alone!'

'Sorry, buster,' I said. 'I hate this as much as you do, but I'm going to have to get you ready for your lord and master.' Taking the halter off the hook outside the front of the stall, I approached him with all the authority I could summon and slipped it over his head before he had time to think out any strategy. He wasn't pleased with that, either. And when I tried to pull on the lead shank to get him to leave, he braced his legs and refused to move. I unhooked the lead shank. 'Well,' I said, 'round one to you. But you're going to have to give in sooner or later.' His ears went back again.

And then I remembered the box of carrots somewhere in the tack room. Something told me that Ransom was not used to treats, and that his owner might well not approve of them. But I was not about to cry uncle and go get help. It would be too humiliating.... I went to get a carrot.

Ransom grabbed the carrot and would have accepted my hand as well to crunch between his powerful jaws, if I hadn't snatched it out of range. I went and got another carrot, simply holding it in one hand. Then I unlatched his stall, unhooked the halter from the wall, and led Ransom out. I continued to hold the carrot, but after letting him catch one glimpse, I kept it out of sight in front of me, while I led him out into the courtyard and fastened his lead shank to a ring out there. Then I gave him the carrot. He ingested that in a few powerful crunches. After that I went to work on him.

Penelope was right. I had to stay alert. Twice

he started to nip a piece of my anatomy, and once I got my foot out of the way of his hoof just in time.

It was while I was brushing his sides that I saw the fresh-looking scars, under the hair of his coat at just about the place where the stirrups would be. Surely, I thought, Conrad doesn't use spurs. I touched one of the scars. It was a bad mistake. Ransom gave a loud neigh, wheeled around and closed his teeth on the back of my jeans. Fortunately, they were loose, and I moved quickly, so all he got was cloth, but I heard the material rip as I leapt out of reach.

'Wow!' I rubbed my rear end. An understanding of why Ransom was as difficult as he was slid into my mind. Another sensitive area could be his mouth, but common sense prevented me from examining that too closely. If I felt I had to do it, I would. But not right after I'd so recently offended him.

'Well, Ransom,' I said a while later, 'you're done. I hope your lord and master doesn't keep you waiting too long.'

'Insensitive brute, isn't he?' a voice said behind me. I turned, seeing the handsome fair-haired boy called Lucian.

'I think he's been treated roughly,' I said. 'Have you seen his sides?'

'I can tell you I'd treat him rough if he were mine.'

I looked at him in surprise. What was it Penelope had said about her son, Lucian? That he was busy with other things. 'You're Lucian Schwartz, aren't you?'

'Nope. I'm Lucian Rattray. My father was number one husband.' He grinned.

'Well would your disposition be that sweet if you'd been jabbed with spurs and had your mouth pulled until it was like numbed rubber?' The latter was a shot in the dark, but I felt it was more than likely true.

'My disposition isn't sweet as it is. And as for horses, I hate the bloody beasts.'

I was thunderstruck. 'Why? Did one fall on you, or kick you or something?'

'I hate them because they're large and stupid and idiot humans spend gross amounts of money on them. We have thirty horses here. Only ten of them belong to us—to the family. The rest are boarders, with owners paying two hundred and fifty dollars a month for full board. And that's cheap by local standards. Places like Devereux charge four hundred. Do you know how many families you could feed on that kind of money?'

I took a brush from out the grooming box and started gently brushing Ransom's tail.

'You know, I can't help feeling it's not the horses you hate, it's something else.'

'Such as?'

I shrugged. 'Who knows? But you don't look to me like someone whose heart is permanently anguished over the poor.'

'What does that crack mean?'

I wasn't sure myself. The words had fallen out before I'd thought about them. 'I think I mean that it gives you an acceptable reason for hating something or somebody.'

'Why don't you try your nickel Freud on somebody else? Like my sister. She could use it.' And he walked off.

I'd finished with Ransom and still Estes Conrad hadn't arrived. I felt a slight twinge of disappointment. Despite Ransom's scars I found myself liking his handsome owner. Perhaps, I thought, somebody else had ridden him with spurs. 'Well, Ransom, I hope he comes soon,' I said. I tied him to a ring in the court and went inside the barn to muck out his stall.

Twenty minutes later fresh sawdust was on the floor, his water had been emptied and refilled, and his tack polished. On my way to my next charge, I passed the open grooming stall and saw Ransom still standing there, tied up. He was now directly in the sun and the flies were bothering him. Picking up a bottle of fly repellent and a rag, I went out, untied him, and moved him into the shade across the court. Then I went to work spraying the fly repellent all over him. 'Sorry about the delay, Ransom,' I said, and went back to work. A half an hour later the sun had followed him again, and he was stamping and trying to toss his head. I stared at him, able, almost, to feel his discomfort and frustration.

Going back in I passed several of the stalls and found Lucian busy mucking out one of them.

'Estes Conrad hasn't come to ride Ransom yet,' I said.

He swung a big fork full of manure into a wheel barrow half in and out of the stall. 'So?'

'So what do you think I should do? Ransom is fidgeting out there and it's getting hot.'

'You're the one who knows the high I.Q. answers. Why ask me?'

'Because I don't believe this garbage about your hating horses. You may hate having to take care of them when you want to do something else. But I don't think you hate them. I don't know why I think so, but I just don't.'

'Ask somebody else.'

'All right. Thanks for the help.'

I went out and had another look at Ransom, untied his lead shank, and moved him again.

Despite the amount of repellent I'd put on him, the flies were still there, and tied up like this he couldn't get away.

Suddenly, out of the blue, anger burst through me. The hell with Estes, I muttered to myself. Without thinking, I unhooked Ransom again, put my foot in the stirrup, and mounted. 'Let's go for a run, Ransom,' I said. 'Get rid of those flies.'

I knew by the time we were trotting down the path, past the ring where John was instructing a group of young women and onto the trail outside that I had started something I wasn't entirely sure I could finish. Possibly Jeremy had done what Estes had asked, and upped his feed. Whatever the reason, Ransom was in no mood to stop. On the other hand, I was in no mood to have him run away with me. A fifteen-minute struggle ensued, during which I cajoled, soothed, and finally fought the big horse to a stop.

'All right,' I said, as he came to a halt, quivering. 'I understand why you feel that way. But from now on we're going to make it a cooperative effort, not a tug of war.'

Letting him know that I was boss, without pulling on the reins, without tugging too hard, and being, withal, extremely careful how I used my legs was not easy. I did not have a crop, and wouldn't have used it if I had one. Finally at the end of an hour, we had reached some kind of an agreement. He was not a sweet-tempered animal, and he was nowhere near the point where I could work with his intelligence. (Because, contrary to what Lucian said, not all horses were stupid, and I was pretty sure that Ransom, behind his fright, fury and rebellion, had an intelligence or an intuition I could work with.) But, I thought, as I trotted soberly back, given a little time and patience, we might do quite well together.

There was a reception committee waiting for us: John Stanton, Penelope and Jeremy.

John approached as I walked into the courtyard. 'Get off the horse,' he said. 'And don't let me ever catch you up on him again. For you he's out of bounds. Estes rides him or I ride him. Period.'

'In that case, which one of you is responsible for the condition of his sides? Somebody bleeds him with spurs.'

John's eyes blinked. 'Neither of us. That's the way he was when Estes bought him and brought him here to board. We don't abuse horses around here. Now get on with the work you're supposed to do.'

Once again I discovered how angry I could get. 'What was I supposed to do with him? I was told to have him ready by eleven. So he was, saddled, in a hot sun, bothered by flies, waiting for his owner who didn't bother to turn up.'

'You could have done a lot of things: taken off his saddle, moved him to the shade, moved him inside—there were plenty of options.'

'I did move him into the shade—twice. What happened to Conrad?'

'He phoned to say he couldn't make it after all. Ransom is the best show horse we have in the stable. And Penelope tells me she has instructed you to ride Rosebud, Mouse, and Graymalkin, and that's it. Those horses belong to the stable and are used for instruction. Leave the others for more experienced people to exercise.'

'And how do you know I'm not experienced?' Given the state of my mind and memory, it was a stupid question. I realized how stupid in a second.

'Because you have been extremely cagey about telling us where you've been, what stables you've ridden with, and how much experience with horses you've had. Yet you ride well enough, and you seem to know something about instruction. So your reticence about your background strikes me as extremely fishy. What's your business here? What're you doing?'

83

'I'm—' I stopped, shaken. The door, the door to my own past, had been partly opened. I could feel it. It was as though I had been in a dream, a dream that would explain everything, and was forced, abruptly, to wake up.

'You're *what?*'

'Nothing,' I said.

'What I'd like to do is give you a week's wages and get you off the place. You're hiding something, and it doesn't bode any good for us.'

'No, John.' Penelope came slowly forward. 'Perdita was wrong to ride Ransom without permission. But I'm part owner of this farm— or at least of the stock. I have financial interests in it, and I want her here. I have something I want her to do. You can override me, but I don't think you will.'

There was a weird silence. I had the feeling that I was in the middle of a scene that had been going on long before I ever came to the farm, and would continue after I had left...as though both of them, John and Penelope, were bound to this place, as central characters in a saga that had gone on for a long time, in which I had no part, and the language of which I didn't know, and that I stood on the outside to observe, and found myself powerless to help...and also powerless to leave.

'Put Ransom in his stall and get him rubbed

down,' John told Jeremy, and stalked off.

Jeremy took Ransom off. I hated to see him go. I liked Ransom. He needed a disciplining but gentle hand, but I had it, and I felt sure we could have been friends. Angrily I turned away and found myself facing Penelope.

'All right, Perdita,' she said coolly, 'I saved your bacon that time. And I did it for a reason. I've watched you with Nancy. The child can ride. I'm sure of it. But with John teaching her, she's lost her confidence, I'm entering her in one of the horse shows, the Paddington Show, in the Maiden Equitation division. Ransom is being entered, too, not only in the Paddington, but in the Burwell. If he does well this season, he can go on to the big shows in the fall, maybe Harrisburg or Philadelphia. But that's Estes' problem. If he wins...well, life could be quite different around here for all of us and the horses. But Nancy could make a difference too. All she has to do is make a good showing, and we'll be ahead. People will send their children and teenagers, and we need the money. There're plenty around here, with loads of money. Once upon a time, there would have been no question. We would have had more than a stable this size could handle. Now—But there's no point going into that.... With money, luck and the right guidance,

85

Stanton Farm can get back to where it was fifteen years ago. And I intend for that to happen. Nancy is going to be well known in horse circles and will be able to pick her show and mount someday....'

'Penelope—'

'Get Graymalkin done and then give Nancy her lesson. I'm making her your responsibility.'

Penelope and I stared at one another for a moment. I felt that there were some important questions I should ask, but I couldn't quite figure out what they were. My feeling that I was seeing only the surface of a complex situation grew stronger. Finally I said, 'From what I've seen Nancy shows no enthusiasm for horses and riding. For all I know, she may even go as far as her brother does in disliking them.'

'And I am telling you that is not the case. Until John took over her training—which I was foolish enough to let him do six months ago— she rode quite well, not brilliantly, certainly, but competently. Then her trainer had to devote himself to...to something else, and John started to work with her. I blame myself for not seeing it sooner. But she's gone downhill steadily. Mainly for her own sake, I want her confidence back. I've seen you with her, and I think you can do it. It will be your main job here from now on. If I have to, I'll hire someone else to do some of your stable work. If you can get her to the point where she can do herself credit at the Paddington next month, then...well, you'll see I won't be ungrateful. We may be strapped for money in some respects, but there's always enough to reward those who work well with us.' Her eyes never left my face while she was telling me this. She never even blinked. I found my own were almost sticking open with the effort to return her steady gaze. I had forgotten what an attractive woman she was—or could be.

'As for Lucian,' she continued, 'well, he has what he thinks is a grievance. His father spoiled him. His idea of the perfect life is to be an international playboy. He needs discipline, and working here is what's giving it to him.'

I said nothing, but it occurred to me that Lucian hadn't appeared to be an aspiring playboy, he'd sounded more like an aspiring radical.

'You notice,' Penelope went on, 'that I'm not asking you awkward questions as to where you trained and so on. Like John I noticed that you seemed much more knowledgeable than you saw fit to tell us. But you can keep your secrets, as far as I'm concerned, as long as you do as I ask.'

It was on the edge of my tongue to say, And

I don't? Because, after all, other than discovering that I had no memory, or not much, what could she find out about me? Unless, of course, there was something....

It was cool, yet a light sweat broke out on my skin. I was aware, suddenly, of being afraid. But afraid of what? Why did I feel so urgently that I did not want her poking around in my past? What was there? Something I didn't want people to know? Or to know myself?

'Is something the matter?'

'No,' I managed to say.

'And by the way. John lied a little. I can't blame him. He does use spurs sometimes. It's true Ransom got most of his injuries before he came here. But John spent a while trying to school him before Estes bought him. Estes is not only a good rider. He's the best in this section of the country. Being rough on a horse for *him* would be unthinkable. ...Get Graymalkin done and then give Nancy her lesson. If John is in the ring, tell him these are my instructions.'

I finally came to life. 'I thought Nancy had a virus.'

'What she has is a slight upset stomach. No more. There's no reason she can't have a lesson. She can rest after that. I'll get her ready.' And she walked off.

I walked slowly back into the barn.

'Congratulations,' Lucian said from the stall he was cleaning out. 'She's given you a nice job.' He grinned. 'A real challenge.'

I stopped. 'She told me you wanted to be an international playboy.'

'Yeah? I guess she likes that better than the truth.'

I looked at him, wondering whether to ask him the question that was on my mind, whether I could trust his answer. 'Since you obviously overheard, you probably heard what she said about Nancy's being demoralized by John's teaching. And about his abusing spurs on Ransom. Is there any truth in either?' Curiously, I'd trust his answer more than his mother's.

He watched me out of his narrow green eyes. 'Sure. So what? What's it to you? Oh—' He gave an unpleasant smile. 'I see. You have a crush on our John....'

'I do not,' I said angrily. 'How could I, since I've never had so much as a courteous word from him? And anyway, he practically accused me of being here under false pretences.

'So did Penelope. Are you? Here under false pretences?'

'No, I'm not....' But even to me my denial

89

didn't carry much conviction. Why didn't I explain that I'd lost my memory? Surely that was better than leaving them to think that I was lying to them for less than honest reasons? But whatever the cause of my stubbornness, I couldn't bring myself to tell the truth. Something was blocking me....

'I'm not,' I said finally, and walked away from Lucian.

'Then why not give us a brief rundown on your recent places of employment. Cops chasing you?'

I knew it was a meaningless taunt simply flung to irritate me. Yet, I found I was hanging onto the lower half of Graymalkin's stall for dear life, fighting panic....

CHAPTER FOUR

And from then on, everything changed. I still mucked out stalls and exercised horses or turned them out into the fields around the stables when their owners didn't show up. But mostly I was with Nancy.

She came down that afternoon, clutching her crop, her hard riding hat somewhat askew.

'Are you sure you feel up to it?' I asked. It struck me that she looked even paler than usual.

'Oh. I'm looking forward to it.' And then, when I continued to look closely at her, achieved a smile.

'If you don't want to ride, I wish you'd let me know. I wouldn't mind talking to your mother about it.'

'Oh no. I really want to. All my friends are going to be in the show. Please do teach me. You'll be so much better than John. He was... he was horrible.'

John could hardly help but hear this, as he was walking Graymalkin out to the trails, leading a group who were practicing for a cross-country course. And Nancy's treble voice carried.

I glanced at him, but either he didn't hear, or he was putting up a convincing act of not having heard.

'Okay, now,' he was saying to the others, 'don't crowd, but on the other hand don't get too strung out.'

'Did you have to say that so loud, Nancy?' I said, somewhat embarrassed. 'He couldn't have avoided hearing.'

'I'm glad.' She showed more animation than I had ever seen in her before. 'I hate him. He bullies me, *and* the horses. If Uncle Max was just alive...'

I helped her onto Bayou and mounted Mouse, who was rapidly becoming my favourite.

'Come on, let's go out to the ring for a while. Nobody'll be there. Who's Uncle Max?'

'John's father,' she said, as we walked the horses side by side out to the ring. 'Mummy's husband. He was wonderful to me, until John turned him against me.'

'How could he do that?'

'Well of course he couldn't really, but he tried. Uncle Max taught me himself and thought I was a terrific rider.'

If Uncle Max had been any judge of riders, I decided, half an hour later, then John Stanton, his son, must have indeed been a destructive force in Nancy's life, because her psychological attitude was successfully concealing any skill she might have. Bayou was far from a difficult horse, but Nancy lacked any remote sense of how a horse would react to her tension in the saddle, her poking heels, and her clutching hand on the reins.

'Look, I know you're a little scared. But there's nothing to be frightened of. I won't let Bayou run away with you.'

'But I might fall!'

'Well, so what? I must have fallen twenty or more times....'

And there, for a moment, in my mind, were the pictures: myself down into the dirt of a ring, one hand still clutching the reins, a gentle bay nuzzling my shoulder...feeling the ground coming up as the horse cleared a water jump... Jingle's astonishment as I came off his back, and my father's cheerful laugh....

'Perdita, what's the matter?'

'Nothing,' I said, again shaken by the memories that had dropped into my head out of a hidden past. 'I was just thinking about times I had fallen. And I'm none the worse for it.' Was it true? 'Now, try again. Keep your elbows in, your hands quiet and your legs steady. And try to sit straighter. You're leaning too far forward. You don't have to rise that high in the saddle. The less air between your breeches and the leather the better.'

'Penelope and Estes said that this was the proper way to post. That it's the show style.'

'Well, they're not here right now, so do it the way I asked.'

'It's pretty confusing to have to learn two ways.'

'You'll survive,' I said heartlessly. 'And besides, I don't think it's two ways.'

But I was wrong. I'd been teaching Nancy

93

for about two weeks when Jeremy wandered out one afternoon, the sun glowing on his already red nose. He stood on the other side of the fence surrounding the ring and chewed a grass blade while watching us work.

'Don't bounce so, Nancy,' I told her. 'Try to feel the motion of the horse raise you from the saddle and sink you back into it.'

'John said—'

'I thought you didn't like John's teaching.'

Nancy retreated into a grudging silence.

After the lesson was over, Nancy, still in a huff, walked Bayou up towards the barn. Jeremy closed the gate for me and said, 'She's got a point, you know. The American riders are overfond of style. The English just sit in the saddle and think that if they get around the ring or the field that's all that should be asked of them. The Americans are more like the French. Their riding is more stylish.' He threw away the grass blade. 'Ye must have done most of your riding on the other side.'

'Yes,' I said as noncommittally as I could. His comment had certainly given me food for thought.

'What hunt did you ride with?'

'Nothing famous,' I said. 'Just the local ones.'

'Aye. Well, I just thought you ought to

know. That is, if you're training her for the show.'

The trouble was, I didn't know whom to trust. I was mulling it over ten days later, rubbing Mouse down, when Estes came in, ready for a morning ride with Ransom. Since I didn't trust anyone, I thought, he was as good a person as any to ask.

'Is the American show style different from the English?' I asked abruptly. Unlike most of the common herd, he did not use the mounting block, but in one swift, athletic movement was up on Ransom's back. I glanced at his feet. No spurs. 'Whoa there,' he said genially, as Ransom pranced around. When he had him still he said, 'Yes. It can be. It's a little dressier, a little more stylish, a little more self-conscious. Haven't you noticed yourself?'

'Yes—I just thought...Well, I hadn't realized that it was actually a different style.'

He grinned. 'You just thought they were bouncing around too much, overdoing things as usual.'

I smiled back. 'Yes—no. That makes me feel stupid, or bigoted, or both, and please don't tell anyone. It's not going to make Penelope happy to know that I've been trying to coach Nancy out of what is considered the approved style.'

He laughed. 'Don't worry. Nancy has improved enormously. I saw her ride in just now. She may not be ready for a ribbon yet, but she's a hundred times better than she was. She at least rides as though she and the horse had the same purpose in mind.'

I smiled back, gratified. I'd had no feedback on how Nancy was progressing the weeks I'd been working with her, and praise was sweet.

'Come along out for a ride,' he said. 'We can go from the trail into the reservation.'

'I can't,' I said wistfully. 'I still have about four more horses to groom.'

He smiled, and it was hard to shake my head. A ride for the sheer pleasure of it sounded wonderful.

'When's your day off?' he asked.

I hadn't even considered. What was it Penelope had said when she hired me? That I had every third weekend off, and one day a week. I'd been here nearly four weeks, and so far had had no days off.

'I don't know,' I said. 'I'll have to ask.'

'You're the most remarkable employee I've ever heard of. Most I've known have their hours and days off engraved in gold on their fronts so that no one will miss.'

I laughed. 'First I have to find out when it is. Then I'll engrave it.'

'And then tell me, so maybe we can ride sometime on one of your days off.'

'All right.' I was a little breathless.

He sat there on Ransom, effortlessly handling him, as the big horse shifted around. 'By the way,' he said. 'I'm sorry about not showing up that day you got Ransom ready. I was suddenly called to a meeting and couldn't get to a phone. I heard you rode him yourself.'

'I hope you didn't mind. He's...he's a good horse. I enjoyed riding him.'

'He needs a firm hand. But I'm sure you have one. Don't forget about our ride on your day off.' He touched his crop to his head in a sort of salute, and then rode off.

'There's somebody named Reverend Mother Julian on the phone for you,' Lucian said, one morning a day or so later. 'Who on earth is that?'

'Just a friend,' I said carelessly, guiltily aware that I had entirely forgotten about the nuns and the convent. I had been working so hard that I had sunk into sleep the moment I hit the bed, and spent such off hours as I had sleeping. The rest of the time I hadn't thought about anything except what I was doing, and worrying about getting it finished in time to get on with the next task. I tried to explain this to Mother Julian.

'I'm terribly sorry,' I said. 'I just didn't think. I've been so busy I hardly know what I'm doing.'

'That's all right, child. This is not a reproach. I just wanted to be sure you're all right.'

'Except for sore muscles, which are now much better, yes, quite all right.'

'And the headaches?'

To my shock I realized that I hadn't had any in the four weeks. 'None so far.'

'Very good. I'm glad. Any memory coming back?'

I was alone in the office, which was a back room in the house leading through a door into the stable. As far as I knew I could not be overheard. But, for reasons I didn't stop to analyze, I was extremely anxious to say nothing too revealing or compromising. 'Yes...and no.' I lowered my voice even more. 'I sort of remember the English bits.' There was a slight click, so slight I couldn't be certain I'd heard it. 'Reverend Mother—I'm dying to come and see you. Would next Sunday be all right? I've so much to tell you that I don't want to get into it now.'

To my own ears I sounded like an hysterical idiot. But Mother Julian obviously got the point. 'That will be delightful,' she said, as briskly and politely as though she were a duchess expecting me for tea.

'Goodbye,' I said loudly, and lowered the receiver. Then I stood there, my heart pounding. Was there anything in the conversation that would give away my lost memory? Nothing, as far as I could think. Was that click part of my imagination, or had someone lowered the receiver—or raised the receiver—of another extension? And if they had overheard, what had I said? What had Reverend Mother said? And why was I so upset? Wasn't it a perfectly ordinary thing for someone to know the head of a nursing convent?

I went back to the stable and started to prepare Bayou for Nancy's lesson.

'Don't tell me you jumped over the wall?' Lucian said. He was cleaning out water pails near to where I had Bayou hitched while I was brushing him.

'Jumped over what wall?'

'The convent wall, of course. Threw off the veil or whatever they wear, declared your freedom, decided to sample the joys of life.'

'No,' I went around to Bayou's other side. 'I haven't jumped over the wall, because I've never been inside it.' Not entirely true, of course, but true in the spirit of the questions.

'I...just happen to know Mother Julian. She used to be a great friend of an aunt of mine.'

'Yeah? Where? I thought they went into the convent at the age of puberty, or something.'

'So? She could still be a friend of my aunt.'

'You didn't tell us you knew the nuns at the convent.' He sounded almost disgruntled.

'Was there any reason I should? I probably know lots of people you never heard of.'

I waited for his reply, but he appeared to subside.

I could, I thought, putting on Bayou's saddle, go and visit the convent on Saturday morning and—my heart quickened—ride with Estes Conrad in the afternoon. He was much older than I, old enough to be my father. But he was nonetheless attractive, and he was the only man who didn't seem to regard me as a menace or a liability and I found I looked forward each day to his arrival to exercise and train Ransom.

But for a couple of days Estes didn't turn up. I was mucking out Mouse's stall when I heard Penelope say to Lucian. 'I want you to groom Ransom and take him out to the paddock. He hasn't been exercised.'

'Why can't Estes exercise his own bloody brute?'

'Because he called saying he couldn't make it today.'

'Then why don't you exercise him?'

There was a tiny pause. 'Because I have other things to do.'

'You mean you don't want to put up with his tricks—like everybody else.'

'No I don't mean that. And keep a civil tongue in your head. I mean exactly what I said. I have other things to do. Now please do as I ask.'

'Do I have a choice?'

'Not much.'

Letting the light, unsoiled sawdust sift through the big fork in Mouse's stall, I wondered what Lucian meant by 'Do I have a choice?' Somehow it didn't match up with the surly, independent boy with the smart-aleck tongue. And then my blood seemed to stop in my veins as Penelope said, 'And keep an eye on Perdita.'

'She's going to see those nuns on the other side of Route Twenty-two.'

'Yes, I know.'

'She tell you?'

'No.'

'Then how do you know?'

'That's none of your business. Now please take Ransom out.'

'Listening on the extension, I suppose. We used to get chewed out at school for that. Even the other kids thought it was a pretty slimy thing to do.'

'And if I hadn't listened on an extension once, just where do you think you'd be now?'

There was a silence. Then, 'Thanks for reminding me.'

As I heard Penelope's feet retreat, it occurred to me I might just say to her, 'Did you listen in on my conversation with Reverend Mother Julian? I heard a click, so I suppose it was you.' By preference, I discovered, I liked to get things out into the open. I must be more pugnacious than I thought, which, in view of my seven-month-long withdrawal after coming to in the convent, was a little unexpected....

I was musing about this when I heard Lucian open a stall near to Mouse's—Ransom's stall, I thought, probably. Then I was sure of it, because there was Lucian's voice—'All right, you brute, let's get this on you'—followed by the sound of hooves, this time trotting down the concrete side.

I went to the door of Mouse's stall to have a look, and was almost swept down by the big chestnut as it headed out towards freedom.

Closing Mouse's stall, I went to see if Lucian was all right. He was sitting on the floor of Ransom's stall, clutching his knee or his shin—I couldn't quite figure out which—his face as white as the washed wall itself.

'Are you all right?'

He didn't answer. I saw his lower lip caught under his teeth. There was a film of sweat on his head.

'Lucian,' I said gently and went over to him. Gently I touched his shoulder. He gave another cry. I saw then I'd been stupid and clumsy. Preoccupied with his face and leg, I hadn't noticed the tear in his thin T-shirt.

'For Christ's sake don't touch me,' he said. Then he threw up.

I went to the tap in the grooming room and wet a cloth. I brought it back and said, 'Let me put this against your face.'

He nodded. And then he said, 'Sorry about that.'

'It doesn't matter. We've all done it.' *Had I?* Yes, in a big stable, when Ponce de Leon had stepped on my foot and then kicked me in the leg. Ponce de Leon...I could see Ponce de Leon in his stall, a large mean grey who rather liked me, most of the time, but who thought I was somebody else because I had stupidly come up behind him without letting him know who I was. And where was the stall? Not in England...I knew that. And right after that episode, someone ripped into me...but I couldn't see who. The blank suddenly wiped out everything....

'Are *you* all right?'

Lucian, still sitting, was a little less white. He was staring up at me. 'Did he kick you too? You look like you've seen a ghost.'

'No.' I found I was shaky. I tried to smile. 'Just remembering.'

'Whatever it was certainly didn't make you happy. Here, lend me a hand.'

I got a hand under one arm and started to lift. 'I was just thinking about a horse I once knew. The one who did to me more or less what Ransom's done to you. And I, too, was sick.'

'Filthy animal. I'd like to kill him.'

'A horse who behaves like that is usually neglected in some way—even by a rich owner. Look, are you okay? I'd better go and get Ransom.'

'Lotsa luck, although I don't see where he could go. The front gate's locked and the gate to the ring and trail probably is, too.'

'I'd better see.'

I went out into the courtyard. Ransom was nowhere to be seen. The front gate was not locked. Who had left it open I couldn't imagine. Perhaps John Stanton. A general all-purpose grudge I felt against him reasserted itself. I wanted to think he was the careless party....

Nevertheless, whoever was responsible, the open gate provided a serious problem. A few yards down the narrow road lay the highway. Images of the various things that could happen to Ransom, a highly bred and undoubtedly expensive horse, made my blood chill.

Running down the road to the highway, I looked both ways. I didn't see Ransom, but hoof marks in the dirt at the edge of the asphalt made me pretty sure he'd gone that route. A further depressing consideration was that he wasn't shod for asphalt.

I ran back towards the house, with no very clear idea as to what I should do. John, I knew, was down at the ring, coaching some young people. Penelope was almost certainly in the house.... At this point in my cogitations I arrived at the front. Sitting there, a key in the ignition, was a jeep. I didn't think twice. I got in, turned the jeep around, and headed towards the main road. As Mother Julian had pointed out the last time I had driven, I did not have a license and could land in a tub of trouble if I were stopped. But I decided not to worry about that. The first thing was to find the rambunctious chestnut.

Rounding another bend, about two miles

away from the farm. I found Ransom, poised at the side of the road, his ears back, effectively blocking the way to a string of cars led by a truck. A man, who seemed to be the driver of the truck, was standing in the road at a safe distance, brandishing a stick. Other people were out of their cars, watching.

'Just a minute,' I yelled. 'Let me get him.'

The man turned. 'Is this animal yours?'

'Yes. That is, he belongs to the farm I work on.'

'Well get him out of the way or he's going to get the beating of his life. D'ya see what he did to my arm?'

'You should have...' My voice faded. There was really nothing I could claim he should have done except called the police, who would probably, in this horse country, have some idea who to call, if only the local vet. But Ransom wore no identification whatsoever.

'I shoulda what?'

He looked just as angry and a lot meaner than Ransom.

'Hold on a minute, will you? Let me try and work with him. He's as frightened as you are.'

It was the wrong thing to say.

'I ain't frightened, lady. I'm mad as hell. And whether you like it or not, I'm going to lay this on that baby.' He took a step forward.

Ransom's ears went even flatter. The whites of his eyes were showing and he gave the kind of neigh that meant he, too, was mad as hell.

'Look,' I said. 'I didn't mean that. Now hold off a minute.'

'Like hell I will.' He took another step forward.

'I doubt if he'll let you get anywhere near him, and even if you do, he can turn and kick you so fast, you'll never wake up. You'll be in a coma for the rest of your life.'

This time I'd said the right thing. The man paused.

'Okay,' I said. 'Get back in your truck.' I looked at the others, standing in a circle just back of the man. By some lucky chance, cars going in the opposite direction had not come along, or there would have been real trouble. But one might come along at any moment, and I wanted to get Ransom out of the way before it did. 'Could all of you please get back in your cars. I need a little space and quiet to get this horse off the road.'

'That's quite a piece of horseflesh,' one man said. He was in jeans and a riding jacket. 'Interested in selling him?'

'No,' I said, my eyes on Ransom, wishing the man would go away.

'Because if you are, all you have to do is call.

I'd get the brute calmed down in no time.'

I looked at him, disliking him. 'No thanks.'

A car approached from the opposite side, and I heard Ransom's neigh.

I stood where I was, in front of Ransom, blocking the path. Around the corner came a car which pulled to a stop. The driver, a woman, looked out the window.

'Need a hand?'

'Could you back a few yards?' There was a short dirt path leading off the road just in front of her car. If I could get Ransom onto that, I could pull him through a gap in the hedge and probably lead him home from there. But it would take time and patience.

'Okay.' The woman backed, and only just in time. A few seconds later another car came up behind her, blocking her.

Luckily, Lucian had managed to get a halter with ropes onto Ransom. The ropes were now hanging down in front of the horse where, with one incautious step, he could step on them and trip.

Blindly, and more out of habit than anything else, I put my hand in my pocket and saw that in this, at least, the gods were with me. My fingers closed over a carrot. Holding it out in front of me, I walked slowly towards Ransom who stood, mean looking and braced, at the side of the road. As I walked slowly forward I prayed that none of the watchers would speak, that no horn would blow and that no new car would come up.

Evidently the powers that be decided to relent. None of these possible calamities took place. I got to Ransom who took the carrot and chewed it up in a few powerful crunches. Then I said softly, 'Ransom, come along now. I'm sorry you're upset, but nobody's going to hurt you...' and I kept on murmuring and talking, as I reached out and patted his neck. I could feel the way his skin quivered that he was tense, angry and frightened. What on earth had set him off? Surely being groomed by Lucian hadn't done it. Penelope's ungracious son might declare he hated horses, but I didn't think he'd be deliberately cruel. Why I was so sure, I didn't know, but I didn't think so. It was always possible, of course, that Lucian had accidentally rubbed against Ransom's sides, or been careless with his hands and brush around there. In any case, I avoided the area.

Talking, murmuring, patting, stroking, I finally got hold of the ropes and tied them up so that even if he took off again, he wouldn't trip. 'Now let's get into that field,' I said quietly, and took gentle hold of the halter above his nose. Miraculously he let me get him across the tarmac and onto the dirt road. Slowly I let him pick his way through a thin place in the hedge and into the field. I had to leave him there to do something with the jeep, and then decide whether I would park the jeep and walk back to it, or tether Ransom and then get back as fast as I could with another horse. But there wasn't any real decision: I'd park the jeep. I tied the ropes around a slender tree growing near the hedge, knotting them as securely as I could (although Ransom, if he took it into his head to flee, could probably have torn the tree out of the ground) and went back to park the jeep.

Most of the cars had gone, but the man who offered me his card and the woman driver were still there.

'Just remember,' the man said, his head out the window, 'I'll give you a good price. He's a nice piece of horse-flesh. With a little discipline he'd do well.'

'He's had too much already,' I said, before I could stop my overquick tongue. 'Thanks for stopping.'

The man drove off with a roar of exhaust. Hastily I looked across the hedge at Ransom. His head was up and his ears pricked forward, but he didn't seem unduly alarmed. Going over to the other car I said, 'Thanks for stopping.

He was in such a state I don't know what he would have done.'

'That horse belongs to Stanton Farm, doesn't it?'

I looked down at the woman. Blue eyes in a weather-beaten face. A shirt and sweater, and calloused work-roughened hands on the steering wheel. But the woman's voice was educated and well-bred. It was not hard to put two and two together. She was a horse owner herself.

'Yes. That's Ransom. He belongs to Estes Conrad.'

Was I mistaken? Did the woman's eyes appear to withdraw? Friendliness had seemed to come from her before. But all I could feel now was remoteness.

'I see,' she said. Then she looked back at me. 'And you are a Stanton? A relation of Penelope's?'

'No. I work there. My name's Perdita Smith.' Funny, my tongue had been on the point of saying something else.

The chill seemed to thaw a bit. 'I didn't know the Stantons hired outside help. They'd always refused it before. John Stanton is obviously too...or was...but I mustn't gossip.' She put the car in gear.

Oh, but I wish you would, I thought. 'They're not easy to work for,' I blurted

111

out, partly by design, partly because the words seemed to be there.

'I can imagine.' She hesitated. 'What are you doing for them? Instructing?'

'No, mostly mucking out the stalls and exercising the lesser horses.'

'You seem to be overqualified for that. You handled that horse very well indeed.'

'Thanks.'

The blue eyes that had strayed toward Ransom, visible in a gap in the hedge, came back toward me. 'Haven't I seen you somewhere before? I don't remember your name, but you look familiar.'

There it was again, and there, again, was the panic that that question brought. And along with the panic, the blankness. Why was I so frightened? Was it simply fear of being found out?

'I'm afraid you must be mistaken,' I said, and could hear my own voice, as though it came from someone else, high, stammering, the accent rather English.

'It's entirely possible. But what makes you so sure? I might have seen you at a show? In fact, that's where I thought I'd seen you.'

Seen from the standpoint of that possibility, my denial was overdone. But again, I could think of nothing to say: my mind was stampeded by the question, my own behaviour and all that her last statement implied. Fortunately for me, I heard Ransom neigh.

'I have to go,' I said. 'Thanks again,' and started to turn.

'My name is Agatha Mitchell,' she said. 'Fairacre Farm. Here.' And she handed me a card from the dashboard.

'Thanks.' I put it in my pocket, got into the jeep and backed it into the dirt road, parking it opposite from where I had tethered Ransom. If this was the only road leading to a farmhouse, then anyone who tried to get in or out would be out of luck. But until I could get back there was nothing else I could do. First things first, and Ransom undoubtedly came first.

It took me a quarter of an hour to approach Ransom, or rather, to persuade him to let me approach. I had originally intended to lead him back. He was not saddled, and he plainly took a dim view this morning of too great a proximity to any human. But, after I'd unfettered him, some impulse made me jump onto his back. 'Okay, okay, whoa there,' I said, as he pranced around. There was no bit in his mouth; the ropes simply went to his halter and I braced myself for him either to do his best to throw me, or to take off in a wild gallop. By some miracle he didn't do either. For a while he pranced around while I controlled him with my legs and leaned forward and patted and soothed. Then he trotted sedately across the fields.

I did not, of course, remember riding bareback, although I knew I had, and knew that someone—my father?—had said that to ride without a saddle probably brought a closer communion between rider and horse than any other way. Not only was there, obviously, one layer less, but every muscle, every reaction of either, was instantly felt by the other.

To return to the barn should have taken no more than a few minutes. We could not have been more than two miles, or two and a half at the most, from the farm. I could see the humped shape of the barn over the rims of the trees, and knew it to be Stanton's because of the conformation of chimneys on the house— also visible. Yet I found myself not wanting to return, and not wanting to return Ransom, even though I knew that to take any longer than was necessary would be asking for trouble.

I slowed Ransom to a walk and then stopped. Then I slid off and decided to see if I could discover what had happened to make him shoot out of the barn like that.

It didn't take me long. I went over him carefully. His sides seemed no more tender

than before when I approached them cautiously. But as I moved my fingers down the side
of his face, he jerked his head free and I saw
his ears go back again. With a lot more coax-
ing, I got his mouth open and I discovered the
trouble: someone had ridden him with a twisted
bit. The corners of his mouth were bruised and
his tongue was cut and bleeding.

'I'd like to kill whoever did that to you,' I
said.

'So would I.'

I nearly jumped out of my skin, and whirled
around.

His light eyes blazing with anger, John Stanton was standing three feet away.

CHAPTER FIVE

'Either you knew I was here, or you're the
century's greatest actress,' he said.

'You think I'd abuse any animal that way?'

'Then who do you think did it?'

'I'd have said you, except for what you just
said. Maybe you're the great con artist. Lucian
said—' And then I stopped. I hadn't planned to
mention him. I didn't particularly like Lucian,

115

but I felt for no reason that I could put my finger on, that he was somehow victimized by both his mother and John.

John's straight brows went up.

'Lucian said that Ransom's previous ill treatment—or what I thought was the ill treatment he received before he came to us—was the result of my abuse?'

'Yes. Isn't it?'

John came over to Ransom's other side and touched his neck and face. I was astonished to notice that the big chestnut, so edgy when others came near him, seemed perfectly content to have John standing there, handling him. Were my suspicions wrong?

'If Lucian wasn't telling the truth,' I asked slowly, 'then why would he lie?'

'I could give you an answer, but I don't think I will. After all, I have no more reason to trust you than you have to trust me.' He turned around and looked at me. 'You seem ready to believe I'd abuse horses under my care for no cause except, I suppose, pure sadism. After all, my prosperity—the prosperity of Stanton Farm—stands or falls on the quality and conditions of the horses here. Why should I deliberately destroy either one—unless of course I get my kicks that way.' All the time John was talking, Ransom was plainly enjoying his proximity, along with the stroking and the sound of John's voice, and was showing it by rubbing his head up and down John's front.

I was baffled. Animals don't pretend. As they feel, so they behave.

'Then if it's not you—and I'm bound to say that Ransom's not spooked by you—who is it?'

'I have long suspected it's Estes Conrad, but I could never pin it down. Until now'—he opened Ransom's mouth and looked at it— 'such injuries as Ransom had, he could have easily acquired from a previous owner, and his skittishness could be attributed to someone accidentally brushing against an old but painful scar.'

Everything in me resisted the thought that it might be Estes. 'But why should he—' I started, and then saw the full implications of what I was about to say: I was willing to entertain the idea that John might abuse a horse, but not that Estes would.

'I don't know.' John said curtly. 'Obviously I'll have to find out. And now, just for a change, let's talk about you.'

'Me?' I could feel the first fluttering of panic. 'Why should you want to discuss me?' I asked belligerently, hoping to deflect him.

It didn't do any good. 'Because there are various things that don't stack up. You came here as a beginner to help out in the stable. I've watched you. You're obviously more experienced than that. In which case, why would you be in a run-down place like this for slave wages when you could earn twice or more than twice what Penelope's giving you at any one of half-a-dozen farms within thirty miles?'

I didn't say anything. This was exactly—or more or less exactly—what Penelope had implied. Plainly they'd talked.

'You must have been talking to your stepmother,' I said. 'She made the same insinuation.'

'It's pretty clear. Are you running from something or someone? And if so, who? The police? Your family?' he paused. Then went on, 'When people have asked you questions, you've given evasive answers or answers that were impossible to check. I don't give a damn, you understand, except as how it affects the farm. But if there is anything about you that will damage Stanton or reflect discredit on it, then I don't care what your reasons are for pretending to be something you're not—I want you off of here.'

'Fine,' I said. 'I'll leave this afternoon. I'm tired of being probed and questioned. Where I came from and what I did before is none of your business. I've done the job I was hired

118

to do—more than I was hired to do. I hadn't planned on trying to undo the damage *you* did when you terrorized Nancy.'

'I did not terrorize Nancy. If I was...I probably *was* too severe with her. I didn't see at first...well, enough of that. No reason to go into it. I'll get Ransom back. You can drive back in the jeep. And for God's sake, next time, don't try and groom Ransom. I've told you that before. Let Lucian do it.'

'Let Lucian do it!' I exploded. 'He *was* doing it. I was brushing Mouse when he went into Ransom's stall and the next thing I knew Ransom was heading out and Lucian was on the ground almost sick with pain where Ransom kicked him.'

'He said—' John stared at me. Then his brows came down over his bony nose.

'He said *what?*' I asked.

John answered slowly, 'He said you were already in Ransom's stall grooming him, when you hit Ransom who reacted and knocked Lucian on the way out. He said that he was coming in to get Ransom away from you.'

It was such an unlikely lie that I started to laugh. 'Why does he tell such an idiotic story? He'd have to know that the moment you said anything to me I'd tell you the truth. And furthermore, you'd know it was the truth—sooner or later. You can fool around about a lot of things, but not about how a horse feels. Do you think Ransom would let me on his back without a saddle if I'd mistreated him? Didn't you see me riding him, while you were busy creeping up behind us?'

John was still scowling. 'No. I came up on the other side of the far hedge. You were riding him bareback?'

'Yes. See?' And without waiting I jumped up on Ransom's back again. He didn't even try to move. 'Come on, boy. Let's show the so-and-so.' And off we cantered around the field. Ransom was quite happy to be running, as long as none of his injured parts was engaged. Also, I discovered, Ransom liked to jump. We had cleared the hedge before I'd really registered that that was what Ransom had in mind. 'Okay, now,' I said. 'We'd better go back. I wish you were mine!'

We jumped the hedge again and trotted back to where John stood. I brought Ransom to a halt and slid off his back. *Voilà!* I'd like to see Estes try that!'

'So would I,' he said slowly.

There was a silence while he stroked Ransom's neck. Then he said, 'If I've been wrong about you, I'm sorry. You're right—if it doesn't affect the farm or your work, none of us has

120

any right to badger you about whatever it is you're trying to hide.' He sighed. 'I can't even flatter myself that you're some spy sent by another horse farm to check out the competition. There isn't any.'

'What happened to the farm?' I said. And then added, 'I realize that's none of *my* business, so if you don't want to answer I can hardly be offended.'

He glanced up at me from under his brows, and for a moment looked terribly young— hardly more than my own age. It was such a change that I laughed. 'You're not much older than I am, are you? I thought...but you always looked so...well, worried, so *responsible.*'

He made a face. 'That's probably because I am.' Then he grinned. 'I'm twenty-two. How old are you?'

'I think I'm about seventeen or eighteen.' I had answered without thought, as easily as though I'd been chatting with Mother Julian.

'You *think.* Don't you know?'

Suddenly the whole pretence seemed pointless. My mind played with a future résumé: *When they discovered I'd lost my memory and had recently been a psychiatric patient, they of course fired me. One mustn't frighten the horses....* Well, I'd been fired anyway. What did it matter?

'I don't know because I don't know anything

121

about myself at all, my age, my name, who I am, where I came from. I woke up in the convent sanatorium about seven months ago, with a broken leg, a broken head and lots of bruises. I'm at a horse farm because I couldn't go on forever living at the convent, doing nothing, and because, when I started thinking about a job, the only thing that appealed to me was to work with horses. I discovered this after I'd taken a ride with one of the nuns and saw some horses. They had a lot more attraction for me than being a secretary or working in an office...' I paused, John's eyes were on me, painfully intense. 'I tried several farms before Stanton, but all of them wanted references—the kind I couldn't give. Penelope didn't. So, I took the job.'

When he still didn't saying anything, I said rather desperately, 'You don't have to believe me if you don't want to—but it's the truth.'

'I do believe you,' he said slowly. 'It's just crazy enough to be true. And anyway—well,' he finished lamely, 'I do believe you.' Then, 'You don't remember anything?'

'Only in bits. I know that I spent a lot of my life in England. I remember my father—and that he's dead. As I said I don't remember my name, or why I was here, in this part of the country.'

Strange. Except for the nuns, and the one prospective employer I had told the truth to out of sheer exhaustion, I had not said this to anyone and I was unprepared for the effect it had on me. My throat hurt and tears seemed to flood up toward my eyes. Some barrier in my mind was breached, only I didn't know which one, or what it meant. I didn't want John to see my tears, so I turned back toward Ransom, keeping my face close to his neck, and once rubbing my cheeks against his neck, hoping to remove evidence of tears.

'I'm going to ride him back,' I said. 'You take the jeep.' After all, if I was going to leave this afternoon, what did it matter whether I did what he wanted me to or not.

But I found that, after all, I couldn't leave. His hands were on my shoulders. 'I'm sorry,' he said. 'And sorry for all the suspicions I've thrown at you. It can't be easy. But—I do believe you. The thing now to think about, is what's best to do for you.'

The doctors and the nuns were kind, and Mother Julian was, I know, attached to me. Yet nothing that anyone had said before had the effect on me that John's statement did. At that moment, when he now shared what I knew—and didn't know—about myself, I realized how terribly alone I felt.

'Don't cry,' he said. 'It's going to be all right.'

His arms were around me and they felt wonderful. For a moment I felt something I couldn't remember ever feeling—safe. Then I turned in his arms and glanced up. There was an expression on his face that I had never seen there before—it was both tender and unsure.

'Perdita—' he said. His voice was husky, tentative. 'I suppose your real name is something else. But to me it's always going to be Perdita. It suits you. I...I like you so much.'

'I thought you hated me, disapproved of me.'

He gave a lopsided smile. 'Both. And both were to cover up how I really felt.' He bent his head then and I knew he was going to kiss me.

I have no explanation for what happened then. I wanted him to kiss me—at least I thought I did. But the next thing I knew I was pushing him away violently. 'Don't do that. Don't touch me. Don't ever touch me!'

The words were coming out of my mouth. Yet it was as though someone else were speaking them. And I was shaking, shaking all the way up and down my body, my limbs trembling as though I were frightened...frightened for my life. 'Don't touch me,' I whispered, and wondered, in some detached portion of my mind, where the words came from and—even more baffling—where the need to speak them came from.

John stared at me, both the tenderness and the unsureness vanished from his face. In fact, it was impossible to imagine that he had ever felt or shown either emotion. Instead, he had his customary remote, closed-off look. And to this now had been added cynicism.

'I see,' he said, picking up Ransom's lead halter ropes. 'You're one of those. It'd be interesting to know which version: either Penelope put you up to turning me on and you couldn't go through with it, or that's the way you get your kicks. There's a name for it and it's not a particularly nice one. You can drive the jeep back. I'm taking Ransom back to the barn.'

I stood beside the hedge for minutes after he left leading Ransom back across the field toward Stanton. Then, to my surprise, I started to shake violently, the spasms quivering through my body, forcing me to reach out and hold on to a nearby tree. After that I felt giddy and sat down under the tree. At least, I thought, as I sat, holding my swimming head in my hands, I was now out of John's sight. That is, if he turned around. But I didn't think he would.

I held my head down between my knees,

waiting for the dizzy fit to pass. Images, faint shadowy shapes, chased themselves through my mind. I tried to empty my thoughts, to clear the screen on which these strange fantasies were moving. But I seemed to have lost all power to do so. John's face, as he bent over me, appeared again and again, and each time it did, there was a shadow that seemed to loom over him from above, blotting out his face. It was a shadow I knew I recognized, but I could not find the key that would unlock whatever box in my brain contained that knowledge.

Once, when something like this had happened while I was in a doctor's office, he had said to me, 'Don't fight the shadows, let them come.' But though I tried, I couldn't let go. I couldn't let the shadows overtake me. When I attempted to, the fear was so overwhelming that I fainted. When the doctor revived me he said, 'Well, that doesn't seem to work—at least for now.'

Curious, until now I hadn't remembered that incident. I had wiped it from my mind. But here, sitting with my back to the smooth light bark of the silver beech tree, I could hear him say, almost carelessly, 'But you're never going to get well until you face whatever is scaring the wits out of you.... Sooner or later, you'll have to find out what those shadows mean....'

I looked up, taking my hands away from my face, and saw that my palms were glistening with sweat, and I could feel the sweat on my face despite the fact that the day was cool. I put my head back against the tree for a moment. It was then I felt the first stab of pain, and knew that I was about to experience—for the first time since I'd come to Stanton—one of the blinding headaches that so incapacitated me.

'I have to get back,' I muttered to myself, and tried to stand up. But now the headaches was really closing in. Experience told me that I would shortly not be able to see, and would remain in effect blind for about half an hour after that. If I could just get the jeep back before the blindness hit...

It was agony walking across the last field and climbing into the jeep. Every movement sent pain searing through my head. If I could manage to keep going I'd have about fifteen minutes, or less, to get the jeep returned before blackness came.

Somehow I did it. I backed the jeep slowly, then went back down the dirt road as fast as I dared. Every slight declivity in the road was torture, and when I had to stop abruptly to let a truck belch its way out of Stanton's driveway, I thought my head would roll off, and almost wished it would.

But I made it back and parked the jeep just in front of the door. Then, walking carefully, I went through the gate, across the yard and into the barn, heading for the stairs that led to my room.

'I want to talk to you,' Lucian said, coming out of the tack room.

'Later,' I muttered between my teeth.

'It's important—as much for your sake as mine.' There was an urgent, almost desperate note in his voice. But all I could say between clenched jaws, was 'Not now.'

I made it to my room and fell onto my bed just as the blackness descended.

The headache was as bad as it had ever been, and left me weak and shivering by five o'clock when the worst of it had finally gone, leaving its usual legacy of a dull, persistent ache. But at least I could see again, and the stabbing pain had receded. Getting up, I bathed my face in cold water, brushed my teeth, and went downstairs, well aware that I'd left at least half my horse ungroomed.

'I take it you weren't well,' Penelope said coldly, when I got to the bottom of the stairs. She had one of her own horses in the grooming stall. 'But I would be grateful next time if you'd let me know. This isn't like an office where it doesn't matter whether your work waits until the next day or not. Horses have to be groomed, exercised, and let out. And if you don't do your share of it, then someone else has to—usually me. And Nancy missed her lesson.'

I knew, somehow, that that was what she was really angry about, so I addressed that first. 'Penelope—I really don't think Nancy likes either riding or horses.'

Penelope turned around, her eyes frosty. 'I've told you—she has been a perfectly adequate rider for a beginner—and furthermore she enjoys it. She was mistreated and humiliated by John and still feels the effects of that. But the rest is sheer nonsense. And she tells me she much prefers working with you to working with John. By the way, what was the matter with you?'

'I had a migraine headache.'

Penelope's mouth, never her most flexible feature, tightened even further. 'I've always found that to be the excuse used when somebody is just goofing off.'

'Penelope—if you want me to leave, I will. Your stepson in effect fired me this afternoon. Why don't I just pack my bag and go?'

I had not taken that line as a ploy. Between the events of the morning and the return of the blinder, I was ready to crawl back to the convent and live to fight another day. I was frightened by the headache, which I had thought had gone for good, and—far more than that—bewildered and disturbed by what had happened between John and me. I no longer trusted my own instincts, which meant, in effect, that I could not, with any surety, interpret John's acts either. It was like finding oneself in the middle of a movie without having seen the beginning, without knowing anything of the plot, and unable to hear the sound track. I really needed to go back to the convent and try and get things sorted out. I turned back toward the steps when Penelope said, 'No. Don't go.' She hesitated, cleared her throat, and went on, her voice less sharp. 'I'm sorry if I sounded harsh. I'm just concerned about Nancy, and about the stable, which looks as though it really will go broke this time. If you'll just take Nancy out to the ring now and give her her lesson, we'll call everything quits.'

I hesitated, my foot on the bottom step. Why on earth did I even consider doing what they asked? There was nothing for me here—no one to trust, and no way to find a key to what would heal my mind. And yet I heard myself say, 'All right. I'll get Bayou and get him saddled for Nancy....' Why? I wondered, going towards Bayou's stall. Why did I agree so easily? Did it have something to do with John Stanton? If so, why had I pushed him away so violently?

The queer swimming in my head that I hated so much started again. I hung onto the bottom of Bayou's door. Every atom of common sense I had said I should leave the farm. But something much stronger was forcing me to stay. Whether it was John, or a strange, growing conviction that the answer to the riddle of who I was lay here somewhere I couldn't tell. And neither boded peace or serenity—or safety.

Whether because of my training or not, Nancy slowly improved. I decided that teaching her in the ring where, more often than not, John was conducting a jumping class at the other end, made her nervous. So I confined her work in the ring to early morning before classes began or late afternoon when they were over. And I took her out on the trail, riding beside her and working, hour after hour, to ameliorate the panic she felt the moment Bayou did anything he wasn't supposed to, or she wasn't counting on.

'He's going sideways,' she shrieked at me one day, as Bayou, taking exception to a piece of white paper, was shying slightly.

'He's only afraid of that paper, Nancy. He's even more nervous than you are, so have a little fellow feeling. You know it's paper. He doesn't know that. To him it's a strange white object that is behaving in an erratic way. Try a little imagination!'

To my great surprise it worked. Nancy giggled. The thought that the thousand-pound creature on which she was perched might have as much fear as herself struck her as deliciously funny. By sheer accident, I had fallen on a device that worked and I kept at it, making up monologues for Bayou as I went along, which kept Nancy giggling and less liable to fling herself on the reins.

John and I avoided each other. Or rather, he acted as though I weren't there, looking past me, through me or around most of the time and only addressing me if absolutely necessary. I hated it, but felt powerless to do anything about it. Every time I looked at him, half perhaps with the idea of speaking to him, I seemed to see a strange shadow behind him. The fact that I knew that shadow was projected from my own mind neither removed nor changed my fear of it.

On one of the occasions when I went to see Mother Julian I finally told her about it. I hadn't meant to, but something about her kind, implacable gaze brought the words out of me before I knew what I was doing.

'You mean you thought you wanted him to kiss you, but the next thing you knew you were pushing him away as hard as you could?'

I grinned a little. Discussing whether or not to kiss John Stanton seemed an odd thing to be doing with a nun. Yet it felt natural. So, I said, 'It feels funny to be talking about kissing a man with a nun.'

'Why? Do you think we should be protected from the facts of life? Oughtn't we to know about such things?'

Put like that, my reservations seemed silly. 'But I feel so muddled. I thought...I really *wanted* to kiss him, or I thought I did.'

'And I take it you want to stay there. You haven't said so, but the obvious solution to your dilemma seems to be to find a similar job elsewhere. From everything I hear the Stanton place is near bankruptcy and sliding faster all the time. Also, you say you seem to know more than you thought you did. By this time you have a little experience and shouldn't find it too hard to get another place.'

'I have the funniest feeling...' I said slowly, 'that if I stay there...I'll find out about myself.'

There was a silence. Then Reverend Mother said slowly, 'It appears very ramshackle to me, and I don't like the sound of any of those people. However, I trust intuitions, and if yours

133

are telling you that your hidden past—good heavens, that sounds like a bad film!—is tied up there, or is discoverable there, then I suppose you ought to stay.' She hesitated. 'But I've heard some strange things about that place—all since you left here. I suppose, because when various people ask where you are, I tell them you're at Stanton Farm, and these odd comments come out. Putting them all together they add up to disquieting goings on: horses that disappear or are abruptly sold. Some queer charges of cruelty...I really don't like it, and I would be much happier if you left.'

'I can't, Mother Julian. I can't tell you why I can't, I just know that I can't.'

She sighed. 'All right. But this much I will tell you. It's a statement that I've heard more than once. Someone at Stanton has a ferocious temper. I mean that quite seriously. Whoever it is is subject to appalling attacks of anger and almost goes berserk. The rumour is that it is young John Stanton. I've never seen him. He may be devastingly attractive. But if there's anything at all to what I've told you, steer very clear....'

As she spoke my heart seemed to squeeze shut. If what Mother Julian said was true, and I had a horrible feeling it was, then it would account for so much. 'Yes,' I said unhappily 'I'll steer clear.'

The little horse show where Nancy was supposed to make her mark in the Maiden Equitation class took place the following Friday and Saturday. I had no memory of attending horse shows. Yet the moment I arrived with the horse trailer on the field, I found it totally familiar.

Nancy and I drove in the farm van while Bayou rode unconcernedly behind, munching the bunch of hay hung in the front of the trailer. I watched Nancy roll and unroll her handkerchief in her hand and said, 'Peace, Nancy. It's not going to be much different from the trail or the ring.'

'But there'll be all those people there.'

'So what?'

'If I do something wrong they'll see me.'

'And if they do, it's not the end of the world.'

'You don't understand.'

I slowed the van down. 'Do you want to go back? We can. No one's forcing you to compete. We can wait for the next show, or next year, for that matter.'

'No,' she said. And she looked as white as a sheet. 'I'll be all right.'

'Are you sure? You should do what you feel like doing.'

'That's not what John said.'

My heart gave a jump, whether because of pain or something else, I didn't know. 'What did he say—and when?'

'Last night. He asked me how I felt. I told him I was a bit nervous. And he said that that was when you should do it most of all.'

I could easily visualize John making this stoic statement. And as I did so, I suddenly remembered...who was it? My father? No, not my father. But someone...a man...saying to me, 'That's when you go at the fence again, Miss ...Miss...Miss'—what?

'Are you all right, Perdita?'

'Yes. Why?'

'Your face looks funny. It's cold but you're sweating.'

I looked in the rearview mirror. Nancy was right, my face was white and glistening with sweat.

'Yes, fine,' I said. And the shadow receded.

Although I didn't let her know it, I was as nervous as Nancy about her competing. She had been riding well—far better than I had thought she could. That seemed to bolster my first idea about her: she had achieved a greater degree of skill than she appeared to, but terror had driven her back to a novice level.

Nancy's class didn't take place till early afternoon, so after grooming Bayou, we took him to the schooling area and Nancy rode him back and forth and jumped him over crossrails.

Various other riders, with their instructors, were doing the same, and I was pleased to note that Nancy was at least as good as a large number of the others. Only once did she seem to panic.

'For Chris' sake give him more leg,' one loud-voiced instructor yelled at a boy who was riding a rather mettlesome grey. The trouble was, his voice shot right out behind Nancy as she was riding by. I saw her hands tighten on the rein. Bayou threw up his head and seemed to fidget.

'Easy, Nancy, easy. Don't pull on my mouth, you're hurting my mouth.' I felt like a thousand idiots going in for that kind of let's pretend in front of a bunch of grinning instructors. But with Nancy, personalizing the horse worked better than anything else. Perhaps it was the gentler association of the trail.

'You sound like Christopher Robin talking about Eeyore,' said a male voice behind me.

I turned.

He looked about John Stanton's age, but couldn't have been more different. What struck me was the friendliness coming out of the square handsome face, with its thatch of fair hair and blue eyes. 'Matthew Shaw, at your service,' he said, and he held out his hand.

I took it, saying automatically. 'Perdita Smith,' and then, 'Well it's a technique that seems to tickle her, and at least keeps her panic at bearable level.'

'Why should she panic? I mean, if she really hates the brutes, why is she at a horse show competing?'

'Because her mother wants her to,' I heard myself say dryly.

'Ah. Yes, I understand. The horse show version of the stage mother.'

'You sound like you've seen a lot of it.'

'More than I like. If you're an instructor, which I am, in a reasonably well-known and well-run stable, then they come around like flies. Not quite as frequently as the besotted horse-mad teenage girl, but almost.'

'I wonder why,' I said, knowing, or suspecting the answer.

'For the same reason they want their darlings in the right school and the right dancing class, all of which lead to the right cotillion and the right young men.'

'You sound like a cynic.'

'I am. About that. It's a shame to put somebody who really doesn't want to ride on top of a horse. Bad for the horse, bad for the rider.'

'Where do you instruct?'

'Devereux.'

Devereux. It was like plucking a string that went past the wall in my mind and hooked onto something that was just out of reach. I could hardly say, Do I know it? Have I been there? Finally, I did say, 'It's near here, isn't it?'

'Yes. Sure—But you must know that.'

'Why must I know it?'

It was like constant risk-taking. What if he said, because you were there only a year ago?

But he didn't say that. What he said, with a grin, was 'Because I thought everyone in this part of the country knew that—everyone connected with horses, that is.'

'Oh,' I said, and this time did not elaborate. Never apologize, never explain, said the old motto.

'Probably that's just conceit on our part,' he said.

'Probably,' I agreed. 'All right, Nancy,' I said, as she trotted past. 'Try that jump again, and keep your head up. Don't look at the ground.'

I expected Matthew Shaw to wander off. But he stayed near, and when time came to go over to the ring where Nancy's class was being held, he went with us.

Luckily, for Nancy's sake, she was one of

the early contestants in her class. I stood beside Bayou while she waited to hear her number called and wondered what I could say in the final few minutes to make her feel less nervous. Because I could see her mounting anxiety, and I was quite certain that Bayou could feel it through her hands and legs. A normally fairly placid horse, he was beginning to shift his feet and toss his head.

Going over, I put my hand on his neck and the other on her leg. 'Nancy,' I said quietly, 'try not to think whether you're going to do well or not. Think about Bayou. What you're feeling, he feels through your body. And in a sense, he's got a stake in this, too.'

She stared at me, her light brown eyes painfully tense. 'What do you mean?'

'He really wants to please you. Why don't you make it easy for him?'

It was a shot in the dark, something to overcome the hardening lines around her child's mouth, the fear reflected in her eyes. 'Why don't you try and imagine that the whole contest is not to judge *you*—but to judge him.'

The ringmaster called out Nancy's number. She was standing in the middle of the field, a straw hat on her head and a clipboard in her hand, and had turned toward the gate, waiting for Nancy.

'Okay,' Nancy whispered suddenly. 'I *will* try.' And she trotted through the gate and into the ring.

I went quickly along the fence and turned the right angle with it, so that I was watching from the best possible view. Nancy and Bayou trotted around, and she rode well. Whether what I'd said had anything to do with it or not, I had no idea. But, opposite me, on the other side of the field, I saw Penelope. At that moment it struck me for the first time how strange it was that Penelope had left the conduct of Nancy's day at the horse show to me, and had not brought Nancy herself.

'That's Mrs Stanton, isn't it?' Matthew Shaw's voice sounded beside me.

'Yes.'

'Has she only just come?'

'I think so. I haven't seen her before.'

'Probably knows she makes the daughter nervous.'

I glanced at him and then over to where Penelope, hiding behind a big hat, was standing at the back of a knot of people. 'You may be right,' I said slowly. Then I turned my attention to Nancy.

How well the judge rated her, I didn't know. But she got through the ordeal honourably; Bayou's jump over the brush jump was neat and efficient. And she didn't hang on the reins or look panicky.

'Well done,' I said, as she came out the far gate, near where I was standing.

'Do you think I did all right?'

'I think you did well. You're going to have to wait until the others have finished and the top riders are announced at the end of this class.'

I hesitated, wondering if she had seen her mother, wondering, if she hadn't, whether I should mention it to her. The decision was made by Nancy saying suddenly, 'I'm so glad Mummy isn't here. She makes me nervous.'

Involuntarily, I glanced across the width of the field to the other side of the ring. Penelope was not in sight. 'Well, now all you have to do is to stand with the others. You'd better go now to the other gate and wait. Do you want to get off?'

'Yes. I think it'll be easier.'

She slid off, loosened Bayou's saddle and led him back towards the other side, with Shaw and me following.

'I'm going to watch from down here,' she said. And took Bayou to the other end of the fence where she could watch while they both stood in the shade.

'You know, she rides quite well,' Shaw said,

leaning over the fence with me. 'I think I've seen her somewhere before, in another Maiden Equitation Class. If I'm right, she's improved a lot.'

'I didn't know she'd competed before,' I said, considerably surprised. 'Her mother didn't tell me.' I paused. 'Do you know the Stantons?'

'Only to see them around horse shows. I haven't met them. But of course everyone knows about them.'

'Knows what?'

He glanced down at me. 'Knows they're on their last legs and sinking fast—thanks to the late Maxwell Stanton.'

'You know,' I said, picking my words carefully, 'I don't know too much about the Stanton stable—even though I work there. You can't help picking up something here and there .... But I haven't liked to ask straight out. So please tell me—what was it that the late Maxwell did that created such financial disaster?'

'Telescoped, he got too big for his breeches. He had been a widower for some time, and had run a modest sort of place—boarding horses, basic instruction and minor shows. They never really made it to any A shows out of the immediate area. He was too soft-hearted for one thing. They had horses there that were too old to earn them another penny, and should have been sold for meat. But they kept some of them on for the rest of their lives, and keeping a horse, even if nothing is wrong and there's no extra charge, can cost a hundred and fifty dollars a month, if not more. If you multiply that by six or eight geriatric animals, then you've got a steady, outgoing expense.'

'Then he met Penelope and married her. The next thing anyone knew, he was buying much more expensive stock—better horses, hiring instructors, and entering shows he'd never been in before. Then all of a sudden he died. John came back from Princeton to take over the running, and the word was round that they couldn't meet their bills. I haven't heard too much about that lately, but the feeling about them isn't good. I don't know John Stanton personally. For all I know he may be a very good guy. But he's been pretty sharp with people who tried to help—offered good money for his horses. And he keeps himself to himself....'

'He's a good rider and good with the horses,' I found myself saying.

'Then it's a pity he isn't a better administrator. The farm was left to him, not Penelope Stanton, so it's really up to him. I think that's the end of this class. Let's see if Nancy will be called back.'

What Matthew had said was true, yet I found myself wanting to stick up for John. 'Well, it can't be easy for John, anyway, and he works fearfully hard.'

Matthew glanced down at me. 'Are you being a loyal employee, or do you really like him?'

'I'm simply stating the truth.' It sounded horribly pompous, but I didn't want to answer that question.

To my surprise and Nancy's absolute delight, she won fifth prize and came trotting out of the ring with the pink rosette and ribbon attached to Bayou's bridle. I looked up at her when she and Bayou were outside. 'Congratulations, Nancy,' I said. 'You see—you did do well.' For the first time since I'd known her, her cheeks were pink and her eyes shone.

'Now Mummy'll know I'm not stupid or a coward.' She slid off, holding the reins in her left hand in the correct manner. Then she planted a passionate kiss on Bayou's forehead. 'It's all your doing, you WONDERFUL horse.' she said.

'And what about your instructor here?' Matthew said.

'Yes, and to you, too, Perdita. Thanks loads.' And standing on tiptoe, she planted a kiss on my cheek.

'Give yourself some credit,' I said, patting

145

her on the back. 'You worked hard. Now let's get Bayou back to the trailer.'

We walked back to the big field where the vans and trailers were parked, passing dozens of riders wearing the knit, tightly fitting breeches that had replaced the looser cloth twill of my childhood..., *How did I know that?* Because I could see the pictures in my mind; the flared tweed jackets, the black jackets, the hunting caps, the boots and jodhpurs. It was like watching still photographs slowly move into a sequence. And I was in all those pictures, except I couldn't see myself in all of them....

'Hoi!' Matthew was looking at me. 'That's quite a trick you have, passing into another world.'

'Sorry, I was thinking about something else. Did you say something?'

'Yes. I said let's take a photograph of the successful contestants here.'

My immediate reaction was to refuse—why, I wasn't sure. But it was strong, and I was about to say no, when Nancy said, 'Oh yes, do let's. Please, Perdita. I forgot to bring my camera. Well, of course, I didn't know I was going to win. Please let's take a picture of Bayou and me. I may *never* win another ribbon.'

'All right. But don't take such a negative attitude. You may win lots of ribbons, of all colours. Where do you want her and Bayou to stand, Matthew?'

'Here—where the sun won't be in their eyes.'

'Do you want me up or down?' Nancy asked, sounding important.

Matthew was watching me. 'You stand closer.'

'Do you want her on Bayou's back or not?'

He smiled at her, 'You can get up if you wish.'

Nancy mounted neatly. 'You'll be sure to get the ribbon in, won't you?'

'Of course—that's the whole purpose. Perdita—come in a little closer.'

'No,' I said. I was standing some five feet away. 'This is of and for Nancy. I want her to be alone.'

'How about a compromise. I'll do one of Nancy and Bayou alone, and one of all three.'

'We'll see. But take Nancy now.' As he aimed his camera Nancy suddenly said, 'You're not going to get the ribbon in that way.'

'Sorry,' Matthew said good-naturedly. He moved a little. 'Now, that's better. Hold still.' There was a click.

'Do you want to take another in case that doesn't come out?'

'I have one film left. I'll be happy to take another if Perdita will stand close there.'

147

'Do come, Perdita. Why don't you want your picture taken?'

'I break cameras,' I said solemnly. It was as good an answer as any, though not the real one. The real one was that I did not want my picture taken. Why? I didn't know.

'Please, Perdita. Mummy'll be so pleased.'

It was hard to resist her.

'I wish you would,' Matthew said. 'I have a horrible feeling that I moved my hand slightly with the last, and I'm not sure it will come out.'

'Then take another one,' I said, angry at being pushed.

It was Nancy, of course, who talked me—or rather, looked me—into it. She didn't say anything. But those brownish hazel eyes spoke more eloquently than anything she could have said.

'Oh all right.' I went over and stood beside Bayou, moving the horse slightly so that there was no doubt in the world as to the reason for the picture. His ribbon showed up beautifully, but in case anyone could miss it, I stood with my finger pointing towards it.

'You *are* silly,' Nancy said affectionately, after the shot was taken, and Matthew, grinning, was slowly winding the camera.

I didn't feel silly. I felt—not exactly frightened. But as though I'd made a terrible mistake.

148

CHAPTER SIX

'I'll send you those as soon as they're developed,' Matthew said, slipping the flat camera into his pocket.

There was something about that camera that bothered me, something my unconscious mind had picked up and promptly hidden, but other than knowing that it was there, I could not identify it.

'Oh oh,' Matthew said, glancing at his watch. 'My pupil is about to begin in the class over there. I'd better go over and watch him.'

'What class is it?'

'Some type of Hunter.'

'All right. Nice to have met you.'

'Come and see us at Stanton,' Nancy called. Obviously, Matthew had made a hit. Or perhaps his charm lay in that he had witnessed her triumph.

'Will do,' he waved, and walked off towards a line of trees that divided the field we were in from the one beyond.

'Can we go over and watch, Perdita?' Nancy asked. 'I've been so concentrating on Bayou and me that I haven't really seen anything. And I'm hungry?'

'That thought wouldn't have anything to do with the ice cream wagon, would it?'

'Oh no! Of course not!' She grinned. And looked more like an ordinary thirteen-year-old than I had seen before. That gave me some idea of how much her failure in riding had affected her.

'All right. Ice cream, and then we can go over and watch the contestants for a while.'

'Bayou won't mind, will he?' Nancy asked.

'Why don't you ask him?'

Nancy dismounted again and spent our short walk over to the ice cream wagon murmuring low-voiced reassurances to Bayou.

We bought our ice cream and then started over the field to the Maiden Hunter's class. Big horses, one or two sixteen to sixteen and a half hands high went past, one black, one a dappled grey, their riders moving with the skill and intuition of long practice.

'They ride well, don't they?' Nancy said wistfully, watching a bay come from across the field. It's hard from a distance to describe how one bay horse differs from another bay of about the same size. Yet there was something so individual about the horse going past us at an angle, that I stopped. Where the sun glanced off the horse's hide it shone a glossy golden brown. The mane was unusually long, as was the tail, and the entire conformation was a perfect blend of strength and grace.

'My God, he's beautiful!' I said, and to my astonishment and consternation felt tears prick at my eyes. The horse was trotting rapidly past, a woman riding him with set face and mouth. She didn't look like Penelope, but she reminded me of her.

The horse whinnied and seemed to want to turn. The woman brought the crop down behind the saddle. Another whinny, and a toss of the head.

'Why doesn't she leave him alone,' I said angrily. 'She ought to control him without the crop.'

'That's what you tell me,' Nancy said. I turned. Thoughtfully, lovingly, Nancy was feeding the rest of her ice-cream cone to Bayou, who seemed to be enjoying it enormously.

'It's okay, isn't it?' Nancy asked.

'I guess so.' And what a distance you've come, I thought. A few days ago horses were the enemy. Now, if Bayou were a bit smaller, she'd take him on her lap. 'Come on,' I said. 'Let's go over.'

It was the most advanced equitation class of the show. Jumps were placed at carefully calibrated distances, so that the skills of both horse and rider were fully tested. Nancy and I took our place along one side, with Bayou nipping a little grass here and there.

'Gosh they're good,' Nancy said after a while. And I realized that at home she seldom had an opportunity to see riding of that calibre. When John Stanton rode he took the horses out. In the ring, he was on foot while he taught. Over by the gate at the opposite side of the field, I saw Matthew Shaw talking to a boy up on a grey horse. When the boy's turn came I saw that he rode extremely well—outshining many of the others. If that was an example of the schooling at Devereux, then they deserved their reputation.

Nancy applauded loudly when Matthew's candidate completed his turn and rode out. But I found that my tension was mounting, not decreasing, as though I had come for something that had not yet appeared. And then the announcer called out another number and I saw the bay again and his rider, the woman with the thin mouth and the riding crop.

The bay came out, circled, and started on its round.

'That horse is not happy,' I said suddenly.

'Why not?' Nancy asked. 'He's doing terrifically.'

And he was, clearing the fences effortlessly, cantering with a nice even pace, taking fences in stride. But I knew by small signals—the quickly suppressed toss of the head, the slight sidle, the occasional pulling on the rein—that instead of the unified, cooperative effort between horse and rider that can be seen in a truly great performance in the ring or the field, there was a battle of some kind, a very subtle battle going on between the bay and the woman riding him.

'She's not riding him properly,' I said, astonished at my own anger.

'How can you say that? She hasn't made one mistake.'

'Because I just know.'

Nevertheless they emerged without a mistake and stood extremely well for the top ribbon. We waited around for the end of that class when the winners were announced. The thin-lipped woman and the bay were called back to receive second prize. 'Mrs William Devereux riding Bandeau,' the judge intoned.

Bandeau, I thought. It echoed in my mind, striking a chord somewhere. Something, a picture, flashed through my memory and then was gone before I could grasp it.

When Mrs Devereux came riding into the ring to receive her ribbon, it was (to me at least) obvious that she wasn't happy: She (and Bandeau) should have won.

'It's your own fault,' I muttered to the woman under my breath.

'What did she do wrong?' Nancy asked.

Put like that, I wasn't sure I could provide an answer. But I finally said, 'She didn't work *with* her horse. She made him work *for* her.'

'What's the difference?

'I'm not sure I can tell you, just like that. But if you go on riding, you'll learn.'

'Oh.'

Penelope's satisfaction with Nancy's ribbon was almost overpowering.

'I knew she could do it,' Penelope said, watching Nancy nail the ribbon above Bayou's stall. 'But let me give credit where credit's due. You've done a terrific job of teaching her.'

'Thanks,' I said.

'And I was right about getting her away from John. He had her so traumatized that she could hardly get on a horse.'

'You were at the show today, weren't you? I thought I saw you on the far side of the field when Nancy was in the ring.'

'I just dropped in for a moment to see how she was doing. But I didn't want to distract her, so I left immediately.'

154

And how do I reply to that? I thought, taking Mouse's tack from his hook and going towards his stall. When I got there, I received a shock. Mouse wasn't there.

'Has someone else taken Mouse out?' I asked Penelope, coming back to her.

'No. We... John sold him today. I meant to tell you. He's getting on and not too many people ride him. He's really too old to earn us any more money. So—' She glanced up at me. 'Yes, I know it's hard, but those are the facts of life. We're getting in some new horses to-morrow.'

I hadn't realized, till that moment, how fond I'd grown of him.

'Who did you sell him to?' I asked, fearing that I knew the answer.

'To Schreig's. I'm sorry, Perdita. But he had to be put down. We need the money and the space. As I said, if you run a stable, that's the way things are.' She walked off.

So, as of this moment, Mouse was probably dead and being cut up for meat. I threw down the halter and went and sat on the bench in the courtyard. After a while, Jeremy ambled out, and stood looking at me in the late afternoon light.

'Wha's the matter?'

'Mouse.'

155

'Ach ay.'

'At least he could have asked me.'

'And who is he?'

I looked up. 'John—John Stanton.'

'The decision was only made this morning. At least, nobody told me till they took Mouse to Schreig's in the van.'

'Did they give him the shot here?'

'No. Or they would have brought their own truck. But that was broken or something, so she took him in a trailer to their factory.'

Nausea climbed up my throat. I thought of that gentle horse, with his grey coat and friendly eyes, and nose, questing for carrots. 'He'll probably be dead by now.'

'Aye.'

It was as though a hand guided me. I got up, went into the makeshift office opening off the courtyard, opened the phone book and found Schreig's number. I was lifting the receiver when a smell of whiskey made me look up. Jeremy stood in the doorway.

'You're daft, you know. The Stantons'd kill you for less.'

I ignored him and dialled the number.

'This is Stanton Farm,' I said, hearing my own voice and wondering who was dictating the words to me. 'I find that my son, John, wishes to buy back the grey gelding you bought today, unless he has been already destroyed. I'll send someone to pick him up right away.' I took a breath and felt my heart beating. 'Is he...is he still alive?'

'Just a minute.' I heard the rustling of paper and men's voices in the background. Then: 'Yeah, the plant's been closed today, our circuits broke. But this is pretty unusual. I mean, I don't know whether we can let you have him for what we gave you. There are additional costs...'

'We'll work it out,' I said, authority in my voice, and wondered where I was going to get the money—and, in fact, how much money was involved. 'My assistant will be by shortly.' And I hung up.

'Ye've got one hell of a nerve,' Jeremy said.

'Yes.' I could hardly believe what I had done. But all I had to do was think of Mouse, and I knew that I would do it again.

'Jeremy, how much did she get for him?'

'A few hundred—maybe two fifty.'

'Where is Schreig's?'

'Just outside the city of Melton. You come to it on the main highway.' He was looking at me with fascination.

'I'm going to take the trailer.'

'Without telling Penelope?'

'Of course.'

'Ye've got the money?'

'I'll write a cheque.' One of the few efficient things I had done since being at Stanton was to open an account at the only bank in the nearest small town.

'And just where are you going to keep the horse when you bring it back?'

'Here, if I can. If not, I'll board him somewhere else.'

'Ye know,' Jeremy said. 'You don't act at all like somebody that's been waiting on other people all your life. You act like you're used to givin' the orders. For a teenage squirt like you you're pretty bossy.'

The same thought was occurring to me. 'I'll get the trailer,' I said.

'You'd better hurry. You never know when Penelope's going to come out here looking for you.'

'I will.' I got up. 'Jeremy—if she or John come out and want to know what I'm doing with the trailer, can you tell them you don't know? Just long enough for me to get Mouse out and started back here. I don't want them calling Schreig's and telling them not to let me have him.'

Jeremy worked his jaws. 'They'll take my head off.'

'Isn't there any way you could just avoid

them until I get back? If it's where you say it is, I shouldn't be more than an hour or so.'

'I'll get drunk. That's what I'll do. Then they can't get a sensible word out of me.'

'All right. Thanks.' His method of foiling them might not be the best possible, but any method that succeeded would, at this point, help me.

Fortunately, I'd parked the trailer with the small van in front, after I'd let Bayou out. And the key was still in my pocket. Also fortunately, so was my chequebook. I'd taken it on impulse to the show in case I'd have need of it.

I drove as fast as I could, gripped with the feeling that the less time I took, the better Mouse's chances were. The factory was easy to find. I swung the van and the trailer into the big areaway and walked into the side entrance.

'I'm from Stanton Farm,' I said to the man in charge. 'I've come to get the grey gelding.'

I could hear Mouse's whinnying from the moment I entered the barnlike shed where live horses were kept. The place sounded and smelled like the death-house it was, and I hated it, with its horses, mostly old and some broken down, waiting for execution. Luckily, I had enough money to cover the amount. I wrote the cheque as quickly as I could, and got Mouse out of there. Then I put him in his trailer, where he could nuzzle the bunch of hay left from Bayou's trip.

It was dark by the time I got back. Opening the trailer door, I led Mouse out and into his old stall. Then I stayed and brushed and groomed him, and got him some feed and hay, talking to him and generally trying to make him feel comfortable. Because that terrible place he'd been was filled with fear and death, and animals, I knew, could pick up such feelings.

'It's going to be all right, Mouse. You and I are going to live a long and happy life together, I promise,' I said. And gave him a carrot. I patted him again and he rubbed his head against me.

Then I went into the house to face the music.

John was nowhere to be seen. Penelope and Nancy had finished dinner and were in the sitting room.

'I brought Mouse back,' I said.

Penelope looked at me coldly. 'When I couldn't find you and tried to get information out of that drunken sot, Jeremy, I gathered you were doing something of the sort. So I called Schreig's and found that you'd been there and removed the animal. How dare you do such a thing? This is not your stable. Such sentimentality is the kind of thing that destroyed this

160

place. I won't have it.'

'That's not what I hear. I heard that buying expensive horses—more expensive than you could afford—is what brought the farm to bankruptcy.' I saw her mouth open. 'And I didn't hear that from anyone here.'

Penelope stared at me, her eyes narrowed. Whether I would have been so brave if I hadn't an ace in the hole, I didn't know. But I had one powerful weapon—Nancy. Penelope would put up with a lot from me, after my enabling Nancy to win her first ribbon. And both she and I knew it.

'And just where do you intend to keep this horse?'

'Here.'

'At our expense? When I've just explained that we can't keep useless horses?'

'He's not useless. I use him, and if I'm to be any good to you, then I have to have a horse always available to me.'

'There are plenty of horses you can use. And as I told you, we're expecting more horses in this week.'

I played my card. 'You have a lot of empty stalls. If you won't let me keep Mouse here, then I'll go to another stable.'

I could almost see the adding and subtracting going on in her head. If I went to another stable, I would not be available for Nancy.

'Very well, you may keep him here. But I will have to take his upkeep out of your pay.'

'My pay is less than the recognized wage *now*. I'll give you fifty dollars a month. After all,' I said, as she opened her mouth once more. 'I was hired to muck out stables and be an all-purpose dogsbody, not an instructor. Instructors get much higher wages. And I know you want me to go on instructing.'

Silence.

'By the way,' I said, pushing my advantage. 'I haven't had any dinner.'

'Food is available when meals are served. Not at other times.' It was a mean advantage, but she obviously enjoyed it.

My brows went up. 'That's a little petty, isn't it? I didn't ask you to serve me a meal. What I'd like to do is go fix myself a sandwich.'

'I'll make you one,' Nancy said, and ran out of the room towards the kitchen before her mother could stop her.

Defeated, Penelope lowered her gaze to her magazine. 'Very well.'

'By the way,' I said at the door. 'Will you tell John or will I—about our new arrangement?'

'I'll tell him. He left here early this morning and won't be back till Thursday.'

How like him, I thought, going towards the kitchen. Give the death order and then depart, leaving someone else to carry out the dirty work.

Nancy was concocting an enormous sandwich of ham and cheese.

'I *told* Mummy how you felt about Mouse.'

'Then I'm surprised she went ahead with the order.'

'Yes, well...' Nancy said unhappily, 'I guess John told her to and he's the boss.'

A sharp comment to the general effect that Penelope had enough authority to countermand any order sprang to the edge of my tongue, but died there. Angry as I was I didn't feel I should criticize Penelope to her own daughter. Instead I said, 'That's a terrific-looking sandwich you're making. Yummy!'

CHAPTER SEVEN

I was dreaming about that beautiful bay, Bandeau, at the horse show. He whinnied and came over towards me, and I was about to get on him, when I looked up and saw Penelope, or perhaps it was the woman who was riding him at the show, in the saddle. She was trying to force Bandeau in another direction, tugging at the rein, hurting his mouth and digging in her heels that I now saw had wickedly sharp spurs on them.

'Stop!' I screamed in my dream. 'Stop! You're hurting him.' By this time she was bringing the crop down on his side, again and again, and I was powerless to move because they were on the other side of an immensely tall wall that in some incomprehensible way I could see through. I yelled and screamed and called out the horse's name, which was not Bandeau, at least not quite. Then I woke up, with my face wet and the pillow below me wet also.

'What's eatin' ya, screamin' like a banshee?' I sat up. Jeremy, clad in a long old-fashioned nightshirt, was standing in the door with a lamp. 'Ye did ought to be ashamed of yourself.'

'I'm sorry, Jeremy.'

'Screaming and jabbering like that.'

I sat up and put my head in my hands.

'Are ya all right, now?'

'Yes, Jeremy. I'm fine. I'm sorry I woke you up. Thanks, by the way, for not telling Penelope what I was going to do.'

'A man can't even have a drink in peace,' Jeremy complained, retreating. 'All this rubbish about horses and bandits and such like....'

'Mutter, mutter, mutter,' I murmured, and then realized I was not alone. My little feline friend, who had come to sharing some of the night hours with me, was cleaning herself (himself?) at the end of the bed.

'I'm glad you're here,' I said, picking up the small body and hugging it. The kitten felt better nourished than last time. I wondered briefly whether it was on account of growing older, catching more mice, or drinking the milk and eating the small dish of cottage cheese and regular cheese I left out from time to time. The curious thing was, I had never seen the kitten in the daylight and had no idea what colour it was. Sometime before dawn I thought it must return to its turf.

Later the next morning the new horse arrived, a handsome black gelding that looked as though it might have more than a touch of Thoroughbred.

'That's no cheap horse,' I said to Jeremy, who, bleary-eyed, was busy grooming Ransom.

'No. He cost a pretty penny.'

Surely, I thought, the few hundred that poor Mouse's body would have brought were not necessary—in fact would be a drop in the bucket—for such a high-priced piece of horse-flesh.

'It's none of my business,' I said to Penelope, who was busy settling her new acquisition into a big, square corner stall. 'But how much did that horse cost?'

'That's right,' Penelope said. 'It's none of your business.'

I grinned. If it weren't for Nancy, I would have been summarily fired, and I knew it.

'Just asking,' I said, and went to see how my Mouse fared. Poor Mouse had been demoted to a smaller stall. But it was still comfortable, and I was busy mucking it out, when I saw Penelope lead the black horse into the courtyard. I loved animals—horses in particular. But I took an instant dislike to this one. Perhaps it was because his purchase was made in conjunction with Mouse's near end.

As I worked, I watched Penelope go to work, finally putting a saddle on the horse's back, and walking him out. As soon as Mouse was ready, I got Bayou ready, too, and then called out for Nancy, to whom I was giving a lesson in the ring.

When we got there Penelope was there, too. And for the next half hour, as I coached Nancy over jumps and in her paces, I kept an eye on Penelope, who took her horse back and forward, over the jumps, around the ring, reversing, changing gait, sometimes trotting, sometimes cantering. There was no question that she was a good rider. And there was also no question that she was riding a fine horse. But there was something wrong between them. What it was, I couldn't figure out. But I knew it had something to do with the difference between those who worked, psychologically, *with* their horses, and those who simply worked their horses. Penelope belonged to the latter group, something I would have pointed out to Nancy —as I had when discussing Mrs Devereux's riding at the show—if Penelope had not been her mother.

'All right, Nancy,' I said after a while. 'Let's go out on the trail.' She was not doing as well this morning as she had done in the show, and I could see what I should have guessed, that the farther she was away from her mother—as well as John—the better she did.

John showed up on Wednesday, a day before he was due. I wasn't aware of his being there until I suddenly heard his voice. 'Where in hell did that horse come from?'

'Mrs Stanton brought him, John,' Jeremy said. 'He got here last Saturday.'

'Where did she get it?'

'I dunno. She didn't say. But the van that

brought it is one I've seen outside the Devereux place.'

I peeked out of the stall I was mucking out and saw John standing in front of the corner stall, eyeing the big black.

'How much did she pay for him, Jeremy?'

'I didn't see the bill of sale.'

'Come on you old so-and-so. You know. Now tell me.'

'I heard tell it was around forty thousand.'

'My God!'

John stood there for a moment. Then he turned around and saw me. I quickly removed myself back into the stall. His cruelty and deviousness over Mouse had permanently alienated me. I had come to think that my sudden withdrawal when he tried to kiss me was not so much bizarre as sound good sense.

'Do you know anything about this?' John snapped at me. He was standing in the doorway. With his brows down in anger, he looked a lot older than his twenty-two years. In fact, he looked frightening.

'Only what I overheard just now. He arrived the day after Mouse was sent to be butchered.' I spoke as coldly and with as much contempt as I could muster.

'Try an easier lie. Mouse is in the stall round that hall there. I just saw him. What are you trying on?'

'As Jeremy will vouch for, Mouse was sent on *your* instructions to Schreig's. I only found it out when Nancy and I got back from the horse show. As if you didn't know.'

John stared at me for a moment, put down the tack he was holding, and stalked along the hall leading to the house.

It was a warm day of summer and the windows were open. Jeremy and I couldn't hear everything, but we could hear enough, especially Penelope's voice, which had a high carrying quality.

'It's no use getting on your high horse, John, the farm and the land may have been left to you, but the stock and cash was left to us both. It's as much mine as yours. If I want to draw forty thousand out of the common account, then I have every right to. We can't make the kind of impression I want to make with a horse costing less—you know that.'

I heard his voice, the bite of iron in it, but not all his words. Here and there I caught a phrase: 'that idiotic will,' 'the stable comes first,' and then, loudly, 'Mouse—what the hell—?' and lost the rest.

I finished grooming the horse I'd been working on, and then took Rosebud out for a ride, and spent most of the ride trying to argue myself out of believing that John didn't know about Mouse's planned end—that Penelope had simply made him the scapegoat. To believe that, would put me back where I'd been, trusting him and liking him more than was good for me—especially since it seemed it would be a lot more than he liked me in return.

When I got back and was rubbing Rosebud down John appeared in the door of the stall. 'Here,' he said abruptly, holding something out.

I looked at it suspiciously. 'What is it?'

'What it looks like, a cheque.'

Then I took it and glanced at the amount. It was for exactly what I had paid Schreig's for Mouse. I handed it back to him. 'I don't want this. Mouse is safe as long as he belongs to me, and I have a bill of sale at Schreig's saying he does.'

'Mouse is safe—period. That...that was a mistake.'

'I'm sorry, I don't trust you—nor Penelope, nor anyone else here. According to Penelope, it was you who ordered Mouse sold to the butcher. Maybe she lied, putting the blame on you when she saw how upset I was. But if it happened once it can happen again. Mouse is now mine. I'm willing to pay for his upkeep out of the salary I get here. Let's leave it at that.'

He stared at me in obvious exasperation. 'The only person more pig-headed than you are is Penelope. Are you sure you're not related?'

'Nobody I've ever been related to or connected with sent loyal old horses to the butcher's.'

'Since you can't remember, how do you know?'

I paused, the brush in my hand. How *did* I know? A sense of depression came down over me. 'All right. No one I've known for the past seven months. And I will add,' I said, emphatically, combing out Rosebud's mane, 'that anyone I'd care to know wouldn't do that.'

'Since you include me in that category, thanks a lot. Why do you stay?'

I looked at him reproachfully. 'You know the answer to that.'

He flushed a little. 'All right. I'd...I'd forgotten about your psychiatric dilemma, and your problem with references.'

'Since you yourself mentioned it only three seconds ago, I have a hard time believing that.'

'Very well. I'm a villain, have it your own way!' And he stamped out.

Later I went and talked the whole thing over with Mouse. 'But I think I was right, don't you?' I asked. Since Mouse was busy consuming a carrot he didn't answer.

After his escapade down the main road, Ransom had been watched closely by both Jeremy and Penelope, and Lucian had been forbidden to go anywhere near him. I dearly wanted to know who had put that twisted bit inside his mouth, but knew better than to ask.

In the meantime, Ransom was again being underexercised. Estes was either away, or his interest in his horse was erratic, and the high-spirited, powerful chestnut was beginning to cut up. Once when the blacksmith came, Ransom almost succeeded in kicking him. Only Jeremy's quick action got the poor man away in time. And when Penelope was exercising him he threw her off with such vigour that she dislocated her shoulder and sprained her wrist, which accounted for the fact that she sent for me one day about a week after Mouse's return and said in the same cold voice she'd been using towards me since l'affaire Mouse, 'I want you to groom and exercise Ransom today. I'm unable to do it myself.'

I noticed then, that she had a sling on.

'All right,' I said, and managed not to ask, How's your arm?

Ransom laid his ears back the moment I went into his stall. He was a chestnut, not a bay, yet there was something about him that reminded me of the horse, Bandeau. I felt that strange pang within me.

'I'm sorry, Bandeau—I mean Ransom. I'm really sorry. Let's see if we can't cooperate.'

With the aid of a lot of soft-voiced talking, slow, unthreatening moves, and a carrot, I managed to get a halter on Ransom and then led him out to the courtyard. Grooming him was not going to be easy, and I thought we'd both do better outside.

Finally, bit by bit, I got him groomed and saddled. I patted him and stroked his neck and kept an eye on his teeth and my feet, which could be squashed flat if he decided to step on them. But eventually he was ready.

'All right, Ransom. Let's see how we can get on.'

I managed to hold him to a trot through the fence, past the ring, but the moment we were across the small bridge that led to the trail, he took off. We had a long, heart-stopping run. I didn't even try to bring him up until he had at least galloped some of the fidgets out of himself. But after a few miles, I started—gently—pulling him up, tightening the rein, speaking to him, stroking his neck and being as persuasive as I could. Finally he slowed to a canter, then a trot, and finally a walk.

'Okay, buccaneer, now let's take it easy.' I let him walk for a while, then trot and then canter. I could feel his nervousness and spirit through my legs. About six months with a considerate owner who exercised him daily and never used punitive bits or spurs would make a changed horse out of him, I thought, and wished I could qualify.

I was returning along another route when, to my surprise, I saw Matthew Shaw approaching on a fine black gelding.

'Hello, how goes it?' he asked, pulling up.

'What on earth are you doing here? I thought Devereux was the other side of the county.'

'Not quite. It's within riding distance, though not on the main road. I thought I'd come over and see how you're doing.'

'Fine,' I said. 'I'm on my way back.'

'Can I go with you?'

'Sure. Unless there's some reason you shouldn't be seen around Stanton. Is there?'

'No,' he said, laughing. 'Of course not. What an odd question.'

'It's an odd place. Who'd know what kind of funny notion they'd have.'

'Well, perhaps then my offer will not seem as impossible as I thought.'

I looked across at him. 'What offer?'

'I bear from the Devereux family an offer to come to Devereux and work there. I told them of your good work with Nancy, and how I liked your attitude in instructing and teaching, and they've just let somebody go.'

I was stunned. As training stables went, Devereux was to riding what (I had learned from Sister Bede) the Yankees were to baseball. The top. I looked over at Matthew.

'Matthew, I'm extremely flattered. Grateful. Impressed. But you haven't even seen me instruct. How could you give me such a glowing recommendation?'

'You forget. I was watching you before I came up and introduced myself. And as I told you, I've seen Nancy before. After you left I remembered where—what shows. And, as I say, Ann and...Ann Devereux is rather frantically looking for a replacement.'

'Did you start to say somebody else?'

'Well...' He grinned. 'Sonny—who manages the various Devereux farms and is also and incidentally Ann's boyfriend. A lot of her orders are orginally his idea, but she bristles if anybody even implies she isn't the total boss, so we're usually very tactful.'

'Was he at the Paddington?'

'No. But I told him about you when he was looking over the photographs from the show. Incidentally, here's a copy for Nancy of the two of you and her horse. She'll be pleased to see the ribbon came out beautifully. And here's the one just of Nancy and Bayou. The ribbon didn't show up as well in that.'

I took the pictures. What Matthew said was true. By far the best picture of Nancy and Bayou was the one by themselves. But in that the award ribbon was half hidden by Bayou's head. The snapshot of the three of us featured me, in mock solemnity, pointing to the ribbon.

'Sonny saw that and asked about it,' Matthew said. 'As I told you, I'm the stable photographer, so they pay for the film and developing, and on small, unimportant things, like wasting film on other people's horses— unless of course they're interested in buying them—he can be stingy as hell. Anyway, he recognized Nancy and was impressed that she won the ribbon—even a fifth place. So I told him about you. And aside from anything else, Sonny's not one ever to pass up the opportunity to miss having a pretty girl around the place. So, Ann came through with the suggestion about offering you a job. You saw her. She was the one riding Bandeau.'

'Oh. Yes. That's one terrific horse.' It was a feeble thing to say, nothing with comparison with the way I felt when I saw the horse. Yet the pang was back. If I went to work at Devereux, I could—perhaps—work with Bandeau. Weirdly, considering I'd only seen him once,

176

it weighed in the balance. It was like love at first sight. Don't be ridiculous, I told myself. And what would happen to Mouse? Dear Mouse, who probably wouldn't even be allowed inside the front gate of Devereux....

'...and he's picked up a lot of points this season....'

I realized I'd not been listening for a moment or so, and missed whatever it was Matthew was talking about. I must have looked puzzled, because Matthew said gently, 'Bandeau—the horse you admired.'

'Oh. Yes.' I was beginning to feel like a clock that had been wound up. 'But I couldn't. There's Mouse.'

'Who—or what—is Mouse?'

I told him. 'And I bought him from the Stantons,' I finished, without mentioning Mouse's dispatch to Schreig's. 'I'm extremely fond of him. He's a great horse—well schooled, good mover, friendly and so on. But I can't imagine that any horse with such undistinguished ancestry would be allowed at Devereux. And even if he were, I couldn't afford the upkeep there for him. I'm sure it's a lot higher than ours here.'

We rode on for a moment, then Matthew said, 'I'm pretty sure that something could be worked out. If that's your only reason, let me talk to Ann and let you know.'

I couldn't think of a rational reason to refuse. If Devereux did prove willing to let me board Mouse at a lower rate, I wouldn't have any excuse then for refusing. At least not one I could mention. There was always the overwhelming fact of my lost memory. Even with Matthew's recommendation, would they let me work there without checking on my experience? No, it was too risky. And besides...besides what?

'I tell you what, Matthew, why don't we just leave it for a while? I'm truly grateful for your recommending me, and working at Devereux would be a tremendous feather in my cap, aside from just being at such a marvellous place. But the Stantons have been nice to me and it seems fairly crummy to leave them now.'

'Okay—but don't leave it too long. Devereux usually has to fight to keep *off* applicants.'

'Yes, I know, and thanks again.'

We rode for about five more minutes in silence. I had the strong feeling that Matthew was put out by my refusal. 'I'm sorry if I disappointed you, Matthew,' I said. 'It was fantastic of you to push me with Devereux.'

He shrugged. 'You win some, you lose some.' Then, after a minute he glanced at me. 'But I was sort of hoping that we could see more of each other, and it would be a lot easier if you were working there, wouldn't it?'

'Yes. But I have been known to have a day off every now and then.'

He grinned. 'What day is it?'

'Usually a Wednesday.'

'How about next Wednesday?'

'All right.'

'Or, if we don't want to wait that long—you're surely not chained to the barn during the evenings, how about tomorrow night? We could go to a restaurant about ten miles from here that's been written up all over—even in New York. It may be in the depth of the boonies, but it's supposed to have a terrific menu.'

'Lovely. I could use some good food. Eating around Stanton is rather basic.'

'Okay. Why don't I pick you up around seven? Could you be at the end of the drive there? That driveway is hell to negotiate in the only car I have to use.'

'All right.' It hadn't struck me as a particularly demanding driveway. However, he knew his car.

'Okay, I'll see you then. Seven tomorrow. Ciao!' and he turned off a trail that led to the right.

I watched him for a moment, then urged Ransom into a brisk trot. Glancing up, I saw

John Stanton riding toward me down the long avenue of trees, and wondered how much he had seen of Matthew.

'Who's that?' he asked, as he trotted up on Malaya, a skittish black mare.

'A friend,' I said, perversely taciturn.

'I didn't think it was an enemy, but it looked to me like Matt Shaw from Devereux.'

'It was. I didn't know you knew him.'

'Sure I know him. Where did *you* get to know him?'

'At the horse show.'

'What's he doing here?'

'Isn't it state land, this trail? I mean, isn't it free for anyone who wants to use the trail?'

John stared at me under those strange, straight brows. Was he always irritable, I wondered, or was it those eyebrows that gave him that bellicose look? 'Yes, it's state land,' he said evenly. 'The reason I asked, since you seem to resent my questions, is that he's no friend to Stanton Farm. Did he come looking for you, or did you just run into him?'

'What is he supposed to have done to you?'

'I see no reason to tell you. You said a while ago that you didn't trust anyone at Stanton. Well, it goes both ways. I have no reason to trust *you*. I know nothing about you. You could have made up this whole story about a lost memory. You could be running from the police, from narcotics agents, from somebody you'd stolen from—anything. And since I know Shaw is hostile to us, I'd be a fool to confide in you, wouldn't I?'

'Absolutely. Don't tell me anything you don't want me to pass on, verbatim.'

And there we sat on our respective horses, glaring at each other.

'Oh, Perdita,' he said finally, wearily. 'Why do we go on this way? You know how I feel about you. You've shown me all too clearly what you think about that. Standoff. All this talk about trust is just throwing spitballs, isn't it?'

Again I felt that odd prick behind the eyes. If he leaned over even a few inches and kissed me now—which he looked as though he might do—would I throw my arms around his neck and kiss him back, which is exactly what I felt like doing, or would I do as I'd done before, lead him onto the last jump and then push him away? I felt as though two terrible forces were battling something out in my head, and that I, Perdita Smith, was being torn by them. Perdita Smith ...but Smith didn't feel right. It wasn't Smith... it was...it was...

Whether I would have caught the syllable, the first letter, that was almost in my mouth,

I don't know. But John suddenly said, 'Oh the hell with it,' wheeled past Ransom and galloped down the avenue, as though he'd been exploded out of a cannon.

When I got back Estes was standing in the courtyard, talking to Penelope.

'Give Ransom a rubdown and let him rest a few minutes, Perdita,' Penelope said. 'Estes found he could come after all, and wants to take Ransom out.'

'But Ransom has *had* exercise—more than enough. He shouldn't go out right away again, not after days *without* exercise.'

I saw the grey chill come into Penelope's eyes. 'Don't argue with me, Perdita.'

I knew by this time that arguing with Penelope when she was like this was useless. I turned to Estes. 'I know what a terrific rider you are,' I lied, perjuring my soul. 'So I know you wouldn't want to ride him again until he's had a rest.'

Estes looked amused. 'I thought his problem was too much energy with too little exercise. It'll be good for him to wear him out for a change.'

I glanced down at Estes' feet. He had on spurs.

'He doesn't need spurs,' I said.

'Don't presume to tell Estes what to do with

his own horse. How dare you!' Penelope said.

I turned to Estes. 'I'm sorry if I sound as though I were trying to tell you what to do. It's just that Ransom hasn't had much exercise lately—in fact, I should have lunged him before taking him out. But I didn't. And now, if he goes out again, I'm afraid he'll strain something.'

Estes smiled and came towards me, reaching a hand out to pat Ransom as he passed. I felt the horse tug at the rein and back.

'I think I know what to do. Rub him down and get him ready for me.'

All this time Ransom was backing bit by bit.

'All right,' I said, simply to get away from the courtyard. 'I'll get him ready. But it'll take me a while.' Angry and repelled, I led Ransom into the barn. As Estes had come closer, I had smelled his breath, and felt my own horror and withdrawal. He'd been drinking, which would account for the slightly glazed look in his eye, and his insistance on riding his own horse when it could damage him. It also accounted for something I had fought against thinking: that Estes himself was responsible for Ransom's bruised mouth and sides and lacerated tongue. I had simply never before seen him that way— under the influence of drink. But now I had and the ugly mystery was cleared.

183

I was quite determined to prevent Ransom's going out again, but I wasn't sure how to go about it. I took my time getting his tack off, then went to get one of the buckets of water that had been left out to get tepid.

I sponged slowly, murmuring as I did so. Then slowly I brushed and rubbed. Finally I decided to get some help.

'Jeremy,' I said, going into the tack room where the old groom was cleaning some saddles. 'I've got to prevent Estes from taking Ransom out again. Considering this is the first day in a while he's had real excercise, he's had enough. And Estes has on his spurs. And he's been drinking.'

'Ye'll not stop him if he's been drinking. That's when he pulls at their mouths and hurts their sides. He's a terrible cruel man when he's drinking.'

'Well, I'm going to stop him, even if I have to take Ransom out myself. Please help me.'

'Ye want to get me fired? I'm an old man. I've nowhere to go. I can't get another job. Ask John. He'll help you.'

'John's out on Malaya.'

'Then stall for time until he gets back.'

'The way he was taking off, it didn't look like he'd ever come back. Isn't there anywhere I could put Ransom, just to hide him for a

184

while. I won't say you told me. I promise.'

'There's the hollow, just on the other side of the bridge, down below the trees. It's hidden by trees all around and can't be seen from the house. But you'll have to get him on the path to the bridge, and I don't see how you can do that...unless you go through the feed storage area there. You could try that.'

'Thanks, Jeremy. Thanks a lot. I won't tell anyone. I swear.'

He gave the saddle a final rub. 'Go through the granary. There's another door there which doesn't show, because nobody uses it. If you can get Ransom through there without anyone knowing, then you can take the path back of the house. If they're in the office, you'll be out of luck because the office window looks onto the path, and I'll not say I helped you. But if you want to take the chance, then nobody'll think of it.'

This time I moved like lightning. I got Ransom brushed and then sprayed with fly repellant. I threw a light summer sheet over him and, praying hard, led him down the stone corridor to the granary door. Luck was on our side. I led him through the granary past the desk to the door I saw outlined in the panelling, then through the door onto the path behind. Whether Estes and Penelope were in the

185

office I could not tell. There was no way, without my going up to the window and pressing my face against it, so I simply led Ransom down the path, around the trees to the bridge, then down through some more trees to where I imagined the hollow might be.

I was right, it was there, and was totally invisible from either the house or the trail. Unless Ransom whinnied, he'd be completely hidden.

'Go have a roll and a graze,' I said, and patted him. To my surprise and pleasure, he rubbed his face against my chest, and then, with a happy grunt, lunged off across the thick grass.

When I got back I had to work hard to erase all signs of our passage to the feed storage area. After his sponging, Ransom's hooves were wet, so I had to hose down the surrounding part of the aisle to hide his tracks, as though the aisle had been washed after a horse had been groomed there, standing between cross ties. Then I dried as well as I could the floor of the feed storage room and pulled some sacks onto the slightly damp spots. After that I went and started to groom Graymalkin in the grooming stall.

I'd been busy for about half an hour when I heard a sound behind me. Estes was standing there, his good-looking face rather red.

'Where's Ransom?' he asked.

'He's not in his stall,' I said, and felt my heart beating rapidly.

'I can see that for myself. Where is he?'

'He's resting.'

Estes stepped into the stall. 'He's my horse, Perdita, and when I want to ride him, then I'm going to ride him.'

'Hanging on his mouth and digging in your spurs, the way you did last time, I suppose.'

'If I think it's necessary. If he decides he wants a battle of the wills he can have it—only I'm going to win.'

He was standing close to me now. I could smell his breath even more strongly and moved back. 'Could you excuse me a moment, I have to get on with Graymalkin.'

'You're not getting on with any horse until you tell me where *my* horse is. I'm not any more liable to take defiance from you than I am from Ransom.'

It was queer. He talked perfectly calmly. It was his eyes that were frightening: blue, a little bloodshot, and curiously focused on me, un-blinking, unswerving. He looks, I thought, as though he'd like to eat me for dinner...or some-thing. It was the 'or something' that bothered me more than anything else.

'I'm not going to tell you where Ransom is.

187

So you can just leave me and Graymalkin alone.' And I tried to go around the grey's nose.

There was the sound of a crack. Graymalkin uttered a wild neigh and reared. I retreated to the corner, but could go no farther. Graymalkin's hoofs hovered above my head.

I closed my eyes and covered my head with my hands, waiting for the blow that would break my head or my neck. But nothing happened. Cautiously I looked up. Graymalkin had come down to one side, snorting and plunging, but avoiding me. Estes was lying on his back, and John was standing over him, Estes' crop in his hand. As I watched, John brought the crop down on his knees, breaking it.

'Get out of here, Conrad, and don't come back.'

CHAPTER EIGHT

I soothed and stroked Graymalkin and, as he quieted, saw the welt on his skin. 'My God,' I said, 'Estes, you have to be crazy.'

Estes was on his feet. 'Okay, Stanton, but you'd better start packing. Your days here are finished. By next month I'm going to own this place.' And he stalked out, brushing his knees and coat as he went.

John came around and looked at the raised skin on Graymalkin's rump. 'He gets crazy when he drinks. He's had a long dry spell, so I guess everybody thought he had it licked. But recently I thought he'd probably fallen off the wagon.'

'What did he mean when he said he'd own the farm by next month?'

'Probably nothing. It was just a piece of rhetoric.' But John looked worried. 'There's no way he could get hold of the farm unless...'

'Unless Penelope's been selling out to him?' I hadn't meant to answer. And it was just an educated guess springing from what I'd over-heard of the conversation between John and Penelope.

'Right,' John said grimly. 'And I'm not sure what the legal position is even then.' He looked at me. 'That's what my crack about Matt Shaw meant, although I don't suppose he really had anything to do with it. But Ann Devereux and that manager of hers made an offer to buy Stanton when I was away once and Penelope was all ready to sell. She couldn't touch the farm, of course, but she could sell half the stock and take off with the money and then I'd have no choice but to sell the rest. Anyway, I got home in time and put a stop to it. But I don't like to see anybody from that outfit around here.' He paused. 'Now what the hell was Conrad in such a rage about?'

I told him. 'You know what condition Ransom's mouth and sides were in when he took off down the road the other day. I've had a terrible time even grooming him. And after I'd exercised him for a long time—following a period of no exercise—Estes wanted to take him out again and looked and acted as though he was all set to have another "let's see who's boss" contest. Anyway, he was wearing spurs.'

All the time I was talking John was stroking Graymalkin, and was putting some alcohol on his backside. 'Well, you acted as I would have. Thanks.'

Suddenly he looked tired and young, and I thought about all the trouble that Estes might cause. 'Do you think...do you think that he can do you any harm, really?'

'I guess I'll have to wait and see.'

'I'll be glad to...to testify, if there's any place to do it.'

John looked at me. 'Any lawyer would get the information about your lost memory out of you in less than five minutes. And I can imagine what he would do with that—any testimony you gave he'd ascribe to an unsound mind and impaired judgment. I can hear his words.'

It was at that moment I heard a slight noise. John turned quickly. 'Who's there?' He paused and went to the door.

I froze, my hand around Graymalkin's nose. But there was no other sound. John came back and gave Graymalkin a final pat. Watching him, a thought from nowhere sprang into my head: What would happen if *I* walked over and gave John a kiss? The idea was delicious. Yet I remembered what had occurred the previous time John had tried to kiss *me*. I thought I wanted it—and then, hardly knowing what I was doing, I pushed him away. Was I unstable? Mentally unpredictable? It was a depressing prospect.

'What's the matter?' John asked.

Before I knew it, I said, 'I was wondering what would happen if I came over and kissed you.'

There was a silence.

Afterwards I realized what I wanted him to say was, 'Come here and let's try,' or for him just to march over and grab me. But that's not what happened. His grey eyes seemed to lengthen the distance between us. 'I have a clear memory of what happened the last time. Lots of come-on, no follow-through.' And with that he walked out of the stall.

I was furious.

My evening with Matthew turned out delight-
fully. When I got down to the end of the roadway and onto the main road, I saw him parked
in a huge old station wagon which justified
his stated reluctance to manoeuvre it down the
narrow roadway. Still, since feed vans, horse
trailers and pickup trucks negotiated the path,
I thought that the bad relationship between
Devereux and Stanton probably accounted for
some of Matthew's reluctance to come up to
the stable door.

'I see now what you mean,' I said, getting in.

'What did you expect me to have?' he asked,
putting the wagon in gear. 'A VW or a Fiat?'

'I suppose so—something dashing and sporty.'

He laughed. 'You have me confused with
John Stanton.'

I looked at him in astonishment. 'John Stanton? He's the least sporty person I can think
of.'

'You didn't know him when I did. He used
to tear around in a Mercedes, belonged to the
hunt club—which is one of the most expensive
in the country—and went to all the hotsy-totsy
watering holes between here and New York,

and some there, too.'

I tried to imagine John Stanton in this role and failed. All I could do was see him in his jeans, or worn riding pants, with clean but equally worn shirts, driving a jeeplike car and, often mucking out his own stable. 'He sure isn't like that now,' I said.

'Well, Stanton's come down in the world.'

Perversely, I felt irritated at this. 'I think they're going to make it. John works extremely hard, and some of his pupils may do well in the next years.' I hadn't an idea whether or not this was true. I simply felt impelled to say it. And then I remembered Estes' statement about owning Stanton. 'Do you know someone named Estes Conrad?'

'Sure. Everyone knows Estes. A good—but erratic—rider. Why?'

'Oh—he boards a horse with us.'

'Ransom?'

I jumped a little. 'Yes. You know the horse?'

'I've seen Estes ride him at shows. He has a horse at Devereux, too.'

I forgot caution. 'In that case—if Estes rides at a lot of shows—I'm surprised he doesn't treat his horses better.'

'Yeah—I know what you mean. Estes is pretty hung up on being boss. And if a horse argues with him he plays rough, although I haven't heard anything about his trying it at Devereux. They sure as hell wouldn't put up with it there. Is John Stanton so eager for money that he carefully doesn't notice?'

'Look—why do you keep making these comments about John Stanton? I like him. He's been pretty good to me.'

'Sorry, Perdita.' Matthew put his hand out for a moment and covered mine. 'Just jealous, I guess. He has you all to himself all day.'

'You needn't be jealous—I don't think he could care less.'

'Stupid as well as everything else, I see.'

I was torn. I wanted to stick up for John for reasons I didn't wish to examine too closely. On the other hand, it was nice having my hand squeezed by someone as attractive as Matthew Shaw. He was a lot better looking than John Stanton, and seemed more my age. So I didn't say anything.

We went to one of the country restaurants noted for its gourmet cuisine. Even I had heard of it. Called simply, 'The Mill', it was near a small bridge over a stream, and the building itself had started out two hundred years before as a mill. Not too much was left of the original structure, but it was rebuilt in more or less the same shape, so that there were two floors. Instead of solid walls, though, great curved panels

194

of glass enabled the diners to look straight into the midst of trees.

After several weeks of Penelope's basic diet of hamburger or stew, the fresh trout tasted delicious, and we lingered until it was dark, staring through the trees to the stream where various walks and small bridges had been placed for strolling.

'Tell me all about yourself,' Matthew said, when we were on ice cream and coffee.

'There's not much to tell,' I replied, on guard again despite myself. John Stanton knew of my lost memory, my blank past. But I felt strongly uninclined to tell anyone else. John's statement about the ease with which people could—if they so wished—dub me mentally unbalanced had had an inhibiting effect. 'The usual,' I went on vaguely, 'school, horses, more horses, and now Stanton.'

I shouldn't have said even that much.

'School where?'

'In the west, a small school you've never heard of.'

'Try me.'

'Babbington.' The word just sprang to my lips. Where it came from I had no idea, but I felt I was safe since I'd just made it up.

'As in Thomas Babbington Macauley?'

'The very same.'

'You're right. I haven't heard of it.'

'Tell me about you,' I said eagerly. It was quite genuine. Aside from my desire to get him off the subject of me, I really did want to know more about him.

'Westchester, local high school, University of Virginia. Am taking a short break working at Devereux.'

'That's a plummy job—working at Devereux. You must be good.'

'I was lucky.'

'Your pupil did pretty well there at the show the other day.'

'He's good.'

'What is Ann Devereux like?'

'What do you mean, what is she like?'

Suddenly, in my mind, I saw the bay horse she was riding, Bandeau. And with that thought came a curious pang. 'That's a beautiful horse she was riding.'

'Bandeau?'

'Yes.' Strange. The name didn't feel right.

'He's a good horse. Pity he doesn't get on better with her.'

So I was right.... 'I saw that,' I said almost eagerly. 'I saw it when she was in the ring with him, and even before that, when she was trotting him over. He didn't want to be there.'

Matthew was looking at me in an odd way.

'You're right about his not wanting to be there. He's been fairly uncooperative since he came to Devereux. Which is a pity. Because Ann's a little like Estes in that way. It's her way or no way.'

'Where did he come from?'

'I'm not sure. Sonny found him. And, as you pointed out, he's a beautiful horse. But either he's not as good as he looks, or Ann's the wrong person for him. It happens sometimes.' He was about to go on when he glanced up, over my shoulder and said, 'Speak of the devil...there's Sonny at the bar over there, with Ann.'

As I turned to look, Matthew waved towards a handsome, dark-haired man in his early forties who was standing at the long mahogany bar across the restaurant. I took in the straight nose, wide sensual mouth and penetrating eyes. Perceptible even at that distance was a sense of power that, far from attracting, both frightened and repelled me, although I could understand its seductive quality. Beside him, looking surprising frail in a long dress, was a fair, youngish woman I recognized as Ann Devereux.

Sonny waved back, glanced at me for a long moment, then, putting a hand under Ann's elbow, led her out the nearby door.

'I guess he and Ann have to get to that party

they were going to,' Matthew said. He grinned.
He certainly gave you the careful examination
—but then he would.'

'What kind of a man is he?' I asked, astonished at the strength of my instinctive recoil.

Matthew took a swallow of his drink. 'Sonny
likes three things—money, horses and good-
looking women. And he's had more than his
share of all of them.'

'How so?'

'Well—he's been married a couple of times.
Both women were rich and good-looking. He's
a gambler and has gone through a big hunk of
his own money. And he knows horses. He
knows them, rides them, and trains them as
well as anyone I've ever known.'

'You sound defensive.'

'There are those who think he's something
of a bastard.'

'Do *you* think he is?'

Matthew made a face. 'Look—he's been
okay to me. Like I said, the Devereux family
has more than one place. Who knows? If I stay
on his good side I could end up managing one
of them. And then maybe saving enough to get
a place of my own.' He glanced at me. 'Sorry
if this sounds opportunistic. But isn't that the
American way? Please the boss and get ahead?'

'Not necessarily,' I said. 'And anyway, that

rather depends on the boss. Is Sonny going to marry Ann Devereux?'

'Probably. Several have tried, but I think he'll do it. Women, old and young, seem to find him devastating. A couple of kids at the farm have made asses of themselves over him—and managed not to endear themselves to Ann by doing so. As a matter of fact, it's one of those you'd be replacing, I hope!'

I smiled as enigmatically as I knew how. 'Is she leaving of her own accord?'

'Well, let's say that Ann felt the girl was spending too much time gazing at Sonny. And I think the kid herself thought that with Ann around—she'd do better elsewhere.'

'You don't make it sound exactly irresistible there.'

'I'm counting on your not losing your head over him, too. Are you going to fall for him?'

'No! I'm not!'

He grinned. 'Well, that puts you in a minority of one—I'm glad to say. By the way, just for the record, can you give me some details of your interesting past?'

My guard was instantly alert. 'Who wants to know?'

'I do, for entirely personal reasons. But for less personal ones, Ann does, too.'

'I thought you said that because of your good

word and Nancy's stellar achievement I was already wanted.'

'That's true. But they do have a sort of administrative office that does have to fill out forms, such as social security and so on. What's the matter?' he went on jokingly, when I didn't answer. 'Don't you have a past? Or too much of one?'

'Both,' I said. And then, 'I had a sort of...of accident.... As a result of which, things are a bit hazy before that. They know this at Stanton, at least John does. But I'd as soon you not go into the gory details for your adminstrative office. If my riding and training Nancy isn't enough, then—well, I'm not sure I want to make a move, anyway.'

'Okay, okay. Sorry. Didn't mean to pry. And your credentials et cetera, are more than enough.' He reached out and briefly touched my hand. 'What would you like to do now?'

'I don't know. What time is it?' I glanced at my watch. It was nearly ten. 'Since I have to get up at the crack of dawn I suppose I ought to be thinking about getting back.'

'No, not till later. Come on. I know a terrific disco.'

'In the *country?*'

'Sure, where've you been? They dissipate here, too.'

I went to the ladies' room while he was paying the bill. It was as I was powdering my nose in front of the mirror, a woman barged up to me, saying 'Pru—' Then, seeing my blank stare, said, 'Sorry, I thought you were someone else.' She had left the cloak room before I could think to speak to her. I rushed out, but she'd gone.

Pru, I thought. Pru...short for Prudence or Prunella...? Did I recognize her at all—even in the back of my mind? The trouble was I wasn't looking at her but at myself in the mirror when she came up, and I got only the vaguest impression of an older woman, perhaps around forty.

'What's the matter?' Matthew asked. He was standing in the hall, waiting for me. 'You look frantic.'

'Nothing really. Just some woman rushed up to me as though she knew me, and I didn't immediately recognize her—I didn't really see her properly—so I was trying to catch her to take a better look.'

'You're probably far more famous than you think,' he said, grinning and took my arm.

We didn't go to the disco after all. The encounter with the woman in the ladies' room had upset me more than I realized, and I intensely wanted to be alone. But what I said was that

I was suddenly tired. 'I'm not used to all this manual labour,' I said, trying to pass it off.

'If you've been around horses, horses, horses, as you say, that's pretty strange.'

It was dark in the car and I couldn't see his face. But his voice sounded a little sharp.

'But then I've been on vacation, vacation, vacation, so maybe that accounts for it. I'll get out here.' We were at the end of the driveway.

'Look, sorry, I didn't mean to sound like the D.A. with a hostile witness. It was just that I was disappointed we didn't have a few more hours—together, swaying around on a hot floor.'

I laughed. I couldn't help it. 'Peace. Another time. If you'll just ask me out again.'

'How about tomorrow?'

'I can't make it tomorrow.'

'Okay, I'll call you.'

I slipped out of the car. 'Do that. Good night, Matthew, and thanks.'

I glanced at my watch by the courtyard lights as I came in. It was twenty minutes past eleven. We'd spent more time over dinner than I'd realized. I stood in the courtyard listening to the typical sounds of a stable at night: stamping, an occasional grunt, and then a whinny. It came from the left, from the smaller stalls, and I had a strong feeling it might be Mouse.

Just for the heck of it, I decided to give him a visit, and took a carrot with me.

Mouse was glad to see me, and when I opened the stall door, came over and rubbed his head against me. I gave him the carrot and stroked and patted him and talked to him for a few minutes in a low voice. A dim night light was kept on in each of the stables, so I was able to check on Mouse's hay and water and the state of his stall. Everything seemed as it should. I gave him a final pat and then returned by the aisle between the stalls to the staircase leading to my room.

In doing so, I passed Ransom's stall and glanced casually in. Then I stopped, unable to believe my eyes. Ransom was down, lying on his side, breathing in a queer, shallow way.

Running to the side wall, I jerked on the full lights, then I went back, opened the stall door and went in.

'Ransom! Ransom!' I crouched down and put my hand on his neck and under his throat. His pulse seemed both feeble and rapid. Then I saw his sides. They were coated with blood, and a bloody foam, dried, was caked around his mouth. 'My God!' I muttered, 'who'd do this?'

I stood up. The first thing to do was to get a vet, and the next would be to find either John or Penelope or even Jeremy.

There was no problem about the vet. His name, Dr William Reynolds, with the telephone number, was mounted prominently up on the tack room wall, near a wall phone. My hand on the telephone, I paused. Probably only John or Penelope had the authority to call the vet, and I should go and look for them. But Ransom's condition argued the fastest possible action. I dialled the doctor.

'What on earth caused it?' the vet asked, when I got him and explained about Ransom.

'Somebody's been abusing him.'

'You've got to be wrong,' the vet said. 'Who are you?'

'My name is Perdita Smith. I work at Stanton as instructor. I've been out during the evening and when I came in went in to check on another horse. Then I found Ransom the way I've just described.'

'Let me speak to John or Penelope.'

'I haven't checked to see if they're in or in bed,' I said, irritated, 'I thought the most important thing to do was to call you.'

'Well you check with them, first. I've had enough trouble with Stanton.' And he hung up.

I stared dumbly at the phone, unable to believe that a doctor would do that. Then I replaced the receiver and ran towards the house.

The downstairs was dark. Turning on the lights, I yelled, 'Anybody home?' There was no answer. Furthermore, the house had an empty feeling. I went upstairs. The first two rooms were empty. Finally I came to a room that fairly obviously belonged to Penelope. Riding clothes were on the chair and photographs of Lucian and Nancy were on the dressing table. But the bed, though turned down, was empty and had not been slept in. The next room was empty. Crossing the hall I entered another room which equally obviously was Nancy's. That, too, was empty, the bed unslept in. Where on earth were they? Probably as a matter of policy, and to make sure everyone knew his place, Penelope never discussed her social engagements within my hearing. And conversations between Nancy and me were strictly about horses.

That left John. No other room upstairs looked as though anyone used it. I ran downstairs again, thinking all the time of Ransom lying there, the queer sounds coming from his throat, and opened all the doors downstairs. I finally found a suite at the end of the wing nearest the stable. I had gone straight past it in my rush upstairs. It was a stark room filled with books and horse magazines, and the minimum of furniture. That bed, not turned down, had also not been slept in. And there was no one in the bathroom downstairs.

That left Jeremy.

I found him, of course, snoring away on his bed, an empty bottle beside him, and I spent a futile five minutes trying to wake him. But even cold water poured over his face and body failed to do more than make him mumble.

I was alone.

I tore back to the stable and put my hand on Ransom again. His pulse was even more rapid. Then I stood up, trying to rack my brains for any recollection of what I must do next.

And that was when the first, continuous memory came back. I was in a barn, a tall horse down, gasping and wheezing.

A woman was there I knew was my mother, and a man, a groom and a doctor, and they were trying to get the horse up. When they failed the doctor poured something...brandy... down his throat.

Brandy. I went back to the tack room, jerked open the cupboard there and saw a bottle of brandy staring at me. Taking it, I went back into the stall.

'Come on, Ransom. Come on, son. This'll

make you feel better.' I prayed I was right. I opened his mouth and poured a little of the liquid down his throat. He coughed and raised his head. Then it flopped back again. I knelt down and felt under his throat again. His pulse was stronger and his breathing felt better.

'I don't know what's the matter with you, sweetheart,' I said. 'But if it's what I think it is, I'd like to do a little killing myself.' Then I poured a little more brandy in his mouth.

Ransom seemed better after a few minutes, so I tried to get a halter on him and then get him up to walk him. But I couldn't manage that, I sat there in my one skirt on the filthy sawdust, and talked gently to him, filled with a terrible rage at whoever had done this to a magnificient animal. Estes Conrad was the obvious culprit, but how and why had he come in? Why didn't John stop him? If, of course, John was there.... And why were the horses left without any responsible person to watch over them? Ransom's pulse seemed a little stronger, but he still had the wheezing noise in his throat and he was still gasping.

Getting up, I went back to the tack-room phone and stared at the vet's number. Then I dialled it again.

'Look,' I said, 'this is Perdita Smith of Stanton Farm again. You have to come. Ransom's

been hurt and there's nobody here but me....'
I was about to say that Jeremy was here but
drunk, but decided—despite my anger at him—
to spare the barn that. No good could come
from a reputation for a drunk stableman.

The man at the other end of the phone seemed to explode. 'This is the second time you've
waked me up. I've had enough trouble with
Stanton Farm. I don't know who the hell you
are; I'm not about to come out on a wild chase
for somebody I've never heard of. If you are
from Stanton, then where the hell are John or
Penelope or Jeremy. Even better, why don't
they pay their damn bills. I have bills too. This
is not a charitable foundation. I thought that
when John got there the nonsense would stop...
but he's as bad as his old man. Now if you
want—'

But I didn't have time to listen to him. I'd
deal with him later. I cradled the receiver,
thought a minute, then asked information for
the number of Devereux Farm. When I got the
farm I asked for Matthew Shaw.

'Who is this?' a man's voice asked brusquely.

'Perdita Smith.'

Silence. 'I'll get Matthew.'

When he came on I told him what I thought
had happened to Ransom and asked him blunt-
ly if he could come and bring a vet. 'I know

that's asking a lot, but I'm terribly worried about Ransom.'

'For God's sake, Perdita, they've got to have an attending vet at Stanton.'

I felt the shame of saying 'He won't come,' as though it were my fault.

'Why not?'

'Matthew—are you going to help me or not? What's important now is Ransom. If you don't want to come, fine, but then tell me somebody who will come. This horse really needs help.'

'Okay, okay. Don't panic. I'll come and will bring our vet.'

'How...how long do you think you'll be? I'm sorry to push—but I'm afraid something's going to happen to Ransom.'

'Will twenty minutes be okay?'

I didn't know whether he was being sarcastic or not, but it didn't matter. 'Fine.'

He and a Dr Mortimer were there in less. I heard them drive up and ran out from the barn.

'Here, over here,' I said.

Dr Mortimer turned out to be a short, stocky, capable-looking man with a fringe of grey hair around his head.

'Tsk tcha,' he said to himself quietly when I took him back to Ransom's stall. 'What happened?'

'I don't know. I found him like this when I came home about...about an hour ago. I've given him brandy.'

The doctor was down on one knee, his stethoscope pressed to Ransom's side. He listened for a minute, then put his hand under Ransom's jaw. Then he looked at his eye, and carefully examined the rest of him.

'He must have been ridden almost to death,' he said.

'Will he be all right?' I asked.

'Yes. But more thanks to you than to me. I think that brandy pulled him around in time. I'm going to give him something for pain, because he must be pretty uncomfortable. And I'll also give him an antispasmodic injection. There you are,' he said, as he pulled the syringe out. 'Good boy! He's a beauty. Who'd ever want to do this to him?'

'I don't know,' I said. 'But I intend to find out. How much do I owe you?'

'That's all right. Young Matthew here said he'd take care of it.'

I really didn't like being indebted to Matthew or anyone else, but there wasn't much other I could do at this point, so I looked at him and smiled. 'Thanks.'

'What on earth—'

We all turned. John Stanton was standing in

the stall door. 'What's going on?' He walked over and knelt beside Ransom, touching him and running his hand along his neck and side. Ransom raised his head and then slowly sat up. 'Good boy! There's a good boy,' John said. 'What in God's name happened to him?' he asked abruptly.'

'Somebody almost killed him,' I said. 'Nearly rode him to death. Thanks to Dr Mortimer his life's been saved.'

John stood up. 'I'm extremely grateful,' he said to Dr Mortimer. Then he turned to me. 'But why didn't you call Reynolds?'

'Maybe we should discuss that later,' I said. I turned to Matthew. 'Thanks again, I really appreciate it.'

Matthew sidled past the two of us. 'That's okay. Glad to be of service.'

Dr Mortimer simply nodded as he went past, snapping his bag closed.

'Just a minute,' John said. 'I'd like to thank you myself for coming here tonight. I don't know why Reynolds couldn't, but I'm grateful for your help. How much do I owe you?'

'Shaw here said he'd take care of it.'

That strange, distancing look appeared in John's eyes. 'There's no need for that. Just send your bill to me.'

'I was delighted to do it for Perdita,' Matthew said.

'This horse is stabled at Stanton, and Stanton is my responsibility. Perdita is simply an employee here. The bill must be sent to me.'

Matthew looked at me and grinned. 'Let that be a lesson to you.'

I ignored him and turned toward the doctor. I was seething with anger against John not only for not being there, and for not arranging to have someone on duty, but for his rudeness. But first things came first, and right now Ransom was first.

'What would you like for us to do for Ransom tonight and tomorrow, doctor?' I asked.

'Don't feed him until tomorrow. Then give him a bran mash—you know what that is?'

'Of course she does,' John said testily. 'Bran, hot water and a little molasses.'

'That's right. Maybe a little wet hay later in the day. Plenty of water. But no pellets or grain. He should be all right.'

Ransom stood up while John was seeing Matthew and Dr Mortimer out. I stood by him, stroking him and arranging his blanket on him. Then I gave him more water, fresh sawdust, and stood there, stroking him.

'Now just what happened?' John said, when he came back.

'Just what happened is that when I came home from having dinner with Matthew, I went to see if Mouse was all right, and on my way back discovered Ransom down in his stall, breathing rapidly and with dried foam on him. I tried to find somebody—anybody. But you and Penelope and Nancy were all out, and when I went for Jeremy, I found him dead drunk and couldn't rouse him. Then I tried to call Dr Reynolds. He yelled at me, saying he had enough trouble with Stanton, asked to speak to you or Penelope or Jeremy, and then, when I said nobody was here, said he wouldn't come out for somebody he'd never heard of. The second time I waked him up he repeated his trouble with Stanton and said—or implied— you didn't pay your bills. That's when I call- ed Matthew. What would you have me do?'

All the time I was talking John was staring at me, and when I was through he didn't say anything. Then he went into Ransom's stall, patted and stroked him, examined him all over, then patted him again and came out, closing the stall after him. 'Go to bed,' he said. 'I'm sitting up with him till the others get back.'

He looked so strained and tired my anger vanished. 'John, who did you leave in charge?'

He looked at me for a moment, then, 'Pene- lope,' he said. 'And of course Jeremy was here, sober. He drinks a lot, but he's never been drunk when he was in charge. Never.'

'Where do you think Penelope went? Nancy wasn't there, either.'

'I don't know, but I can guess. There's a sort of ball going on for a lot of the show people. It's at the inn in the village for the benefit of the humane society or something. Very select. None of us got invitations, which sort of surprised me. But I have more crucial things to worry about than that. I knew it bothered Penelope. She must have wangled an invitation somehow—and one for Nancy.'

'Isn't she a little young for that kind of thing?'

'Not for Penelope's purposes. Social ambition is her middle name. If she can marry Nancy off to some rich horsey landowner or squire she'll die happy. And thirteen is not too young to begin getting her into the right set. Why do you think she pushes the child to ride? And why else do you think she married my father?'

'Where does she come from? Why the obsession?'

'She came from a small New England town. A rich relative sent her to a posh boarding school, thinking to do her a favour. When she got there she realized she had two ordinary sweaters to everybody else's ten cashmeres, but she got to know all the people in the horsey sets of New England, Westchester and Pennsylvania. When she left she had to go to work, and she started in one of the big department stores. It was during those years she picked up husbands number one and two, and got rid of them. Or they got rid of her. Anyway, being smart, she worked her way up, but she never let go of her old contacts, and when she finally got a job managing one of the really exclusive sporty type stores in the middle of horse country, she was back in—as much as she could be. There she met my father who was really more of a working farmer than a squire.... As they say, the rest is history.'

There was so much bitterness in his voice that I was tempted to reach out and pat him, the way I would Ransom. But I also had a feeling that in addition to worry and anger, he was suffering from lacerated pride, and wouldn't appreciate it. Instead I said, 'What kind of man was your father?'

'Sweet, kind, hardworking. We had horses, of course, and rode in local shows and boarded horses belonging to other people. But he never sold an old horse. There was one—Dandy— born long before I was, who lived thirty-nine happy years at Stanton, and died peacefully, standing up, watching kids put up fences. And

Dad was a patsy about taking in others when he thought they were abused. There was a horse named Pete that he bought when it was on its way to the slaughterhouse. It was a foal— only a few months old, but had been so neglected and deprived of proper care that it was almost a skeleton. My father happened to see it when the van stopped here for something— to deliver some feed sacks that had been dropped by the regular deliverer or something. Dad promptly bought the foal, and started taking care of it. At the end of a few months it was a terrific colt. I grew up with it. That horse could have never earned another penny for the farm for the rest of its life, and Dad would have kept it and fed it and turned it out into the pasture and generally spoiled it as long as it lived. It was like a dog when he was around. If the stall door was open it would follow him around the barn. If Dad walked to the fence before calling him home, he'd whinny from two fields over and come running....'

John stopped abruptly and turned away, walking down the hall to the central grooming area. 'Go to bed,' he said over his shoulder.

I stood there, watching him in the dim light, and saw him sit down on a bench. After a minute he put his elbows on his knees and his head in his hands.

I had every intention of doing just what he told me—go upstairs to bed. Heaven knew I was tired enough. Or should have been. I was therefore astonished to find myself walking slowly down the hall to the grooming area to stand in front of him.

'John,' I said.

'Go away,' he said.

I put my hands on his head. He looked up then, and I could see the tears in his eyes. I knelt down and put my arms around him. His arms closed around the back of me and his cheek was against mine. I hugged him hard and he almost broke my ribs. Then he pulled his cheek away and kissed me...and kissed me again. And I kissed him back....

A while later we were both sitting on the bench side by side, and he was holding my hands. Neither of us had said anything for a long while.

'About the bills,' he said finally. 'I didn't know about that. Penelope's always done that. She wanted to handle the business end, so—I let her. I guess that's where she got the money to buy that new horse. By not paying the vet's and other bills. Godalmighty—' He put his other hand up to his head. 'Poor Dad would roll around in his grave. But it sure accounts for some of the queer looks we've been getting.'

'Why would she do that? I mean—if Stanton half belongs to her wouldn't she suffer, too?'

'That's what I've told myself for the past year. When something's happened that I didn't like, I'd tell myself that in the long run her interests were the same—the good of the farm. Now I know it's not so. But I'm damned if I can see why. If the place goes bankrupt, she'll be hurt—at least financially, as much as I. Even when she—' He stopped.

'When she what?'

He didn't say anything. I had the strong feeling that he was trying to decide whether or not to tell me something but at that moment there was the sound of a car being driven up and Penelope's voice, thanking someone, was heard.

John got up, and walked through the courtyard, with me following. Then he turned left at the gate and accosted Penelope just as she was about to open the front door. Both she and Nancy were in long dresses, Nancy's a lacy white floating wide over ruffles.

'Who did you leave in charge of the stable, Penelope?' John said, his voice grating.

Penelope turned, revealing a dark-coloured evening dress cut wide over her shoulders.

With her fine figure, she seemed the height of elegance. Her dark hair was in a twist, and she had on a double strand of pearls.

'Oh good evening, John. I left Jeremy in charge. Why?'

'Because Jeremy is dead drunk and someone almost killed Ransom.'

There was a silence, except for a little gasp from Nancy. Penelope stood like a stone, her mouth narrow. Then she said, 'Where is Perdita?—she always had it in for that horse.'

'I'm here, Penelope, and would never, never under any circumstances abuse a horse—any more than I'd send a much loved pet to the butcher, the way you did Mouse.'

'We have only your word—'

'Oh no we don't. Matthew Shaw brought me home from dinner ten minutes before I found Ransom, and only a few minutes more before I called him back.'

She blinked. 'I didn't know you knew Matthew Shaw.'

'Yes, Mummy,' Nancy said. 'I told you, he was very nice to us at the show.'

Without turning her head, Penelope said, 'You didn't tell me his name. I didn't know it was young Shaw.' Her gaze fixed on John. 'Well, John, your temper is pretty well known....' There was something in her voice

219

that made my flesh crawl.

'Luckily for me,' John said, 'I, too, can prove where I was to within a few minutes of my arriving here, and with whom.'

Penelope shrugged. 'Then Jeremy must have had too much to drink. I told you to get rid of him a year ago when your father died.'

'Jeremy drinks too much. But he's never been drunk on duty before; he cares about horses too much.'

'Then we don't know who it is, do we? And if the horse is all right, what difference does it make?' She started to go in.

'Mummy!' That was Nancy, shocked.

'Go in at once and go to bed. You have to start practicing again in the morning. I've entered you for the Novice class up in the Paddington next week.'

'I can't do that, Mummy. It's too hard. I'll do the Maiden Equitation again.'

'You'll do as I say. Now go in.'

John spoke up, 'Just a minute, Penelope, we're not through yet.'

'Oh yes we are. The subject is closed.'

'No, it isn't. I don't care what you think you have on me, we're going to talk about this right now. Perdita called Reynolds who refused to come on the grounds that we haven't paid our bills. The business end has been in your hands—why the hell haven't we paid our accounts?'

'Because I had other plans for the money. They'll get paid—eventually. Now stand aside. I'm going to bed.'

'Are you crazy? They won't get paid eventually. And what does eventually mean? Our suppliers—to say nothing of the vet—can just stop doing business with us. More important, my father had a fine reputation as long as he lived. I'm not going to have his name—which is my name—destroyed to satisfy some weird ambition of yours. The horse you bought goes back and we pay our bills. Tomorrow!'

Penelope stepped in front of Nancy, facing John. 'Now you listen to me. I can send you to jail. You know it and I know it. I have the proof. And if you do one thing that you've threatened, I'll do it.'

'Go ahead. I'll take my chances with any court. That horse goes back. I'm taking him back myself.'

Evidently she wasn't expecting that answer. There was, for the first time, a look of hesitation on her face. 'We'll see about that—after the Paddington.'

'We can see about anything you please after the Paddington. But that new black horse gets resold tomorrow. And we pay our bills.'

Penelope continued to stare, then she turned around and went into the house.

'Can she put you in jail?' I asked.

John looked at me as though the previous half-hour between us hadn't happened. As though I were a stranger. 'Yes,' he said. 'She can.'

'What...?' I started. And then, because of the bleak remoteness of his face. 'John...'

'Look—' he said, his voice harsh. 'Let's forget...let's forget what happened back there in the stable. Just forget it, Perdita.'

'No. I won't.'

'Yes you will. Because I already have.' And he walked off into a side entrance into the house.

CHAPTER NINE

I didn't go to sleep until nearly three o'clock that night, despite the comforting presence of my furry friend whom I had named Cassandra, for reasons known only to my unconscious mind. I still had never seen her in daylight. She made her presence known, and her desire to join me, on the other side of the door leading to the hayloft, nearly always after I had put out the light. Once I had let her in before I had turned out the dim, low-watt bulb hanging in the middle of my loft. In that highly unreliable light she had looked multicoloured. But what the actual nature of the colours were, it was impossible to tell.

Anyway, I let her in before getting into bed, and spent the next several hours either stroking her, letting her lie on my chest, or feeling her purr in the middle of my back, depending on which position I was in as I twisted and turned.

As I flopped this way and that, the increasing mysteries in my life seemed to march across my mind like great question marks. Who was I? Who rode Ransom in such a diabolical fashion? For what crimes could Penelope have John put in jail?

And of the three the one that tormented me most during the small black hours was the last. I knew by this time that I would trust his integrity to the moon and back. I could not imagine him stealing or lying. Unfortunately, I could imagine him losing his highly losable temper and doing something violent. Hadn't Mother Julian said, 'There's someone at Stanton who has a terrible anger?' Theoretically, he could have been the one, in a fit of rage, to ride Ransom too hard. But not tonight. And anyway, I simply could no longer believe he would do such a thing. I did not believe that whatever his violence, it would be directed against an animal. Which left a wide range of human beings to whom he could very well have directed it.

As to who hurt Ransom? It couldn't be any other than Estes Conrad. How or why or under what circumstances, I did not know. But I was certainly going to find out.

And as to my own identity... More and more of it had come back, disconnected, out of any kind of sequence, I was sure, but they were separate scenes, some in England and some—also among stables and horses and in green fields—that I knew were in America, although I wasn't sure, as yet, where. There was my father. Not only could my mind and vision remember him. My emotions did, too. And when I thought of him, it was hard not to cry. I was pretty sure, without being able to tell why, that he had been dead a number of years .... There was my mother... I could see her face quite clearly, mostly in the American scenes. But my emotions didn't remember her. I saw her face in my inner eye, and nothing whatever happened to my feeling. It was as though she had no connection with me...as though something were barring the way.... But the more

224

I tried to make sense of the bits and pieces that were clear, the less they made sequential sense. It was better to give up. I remembered more when I tried less.

Finally, sometime after a clock somewhere struck three, I drifted off into sleep. This time I was running, running as fast as I could, fleeing with all my strength from something pursuing me. Or was I running toward something? I couldn't be sure. But suddenly, when I thought I was safe, the huge black horse appeared in front of me, rearing, its hooves above my head, and I knew the rider was going to bring it down on top of me....

I awoke to feel someone shaking my shoulder, and to the smell of sour whiskey.

'Stop that noise! Ye'll rouse the house, screaming like that!'

I looked up. Jeremy's unlovely face and alcoholic breath were right above me. I shot up, almost hitting him. 'It was the horse, the black horse. It almost crushed me!'

'Ye're talking a lot of nonsense. Can't you let a man get some sleep? And with a head like mine...'

I remembered then the night before. 'Jeremy,' I said, gripping his arm. 'Who rode Ransom last night?'

'Nobody. Don't be daft. Who'd ride him in

the middle of the night?'

I went about it another way. 'Was Estes here?'

'Ay—looking for you too see if you wanted a spot of dinner.'

'Then what happened?'

'What do you mean what happened? I told him ye'd already gone out. So he left.'

'He left immediately? Or did he stay for a drink with you?'

'It's tired I'm getting of this temperance lecture, I'll have you know. I can take better care of horses, drunk, than you can sober, or will do, at least for the next thirty years.'

'Jeremy, don't get angry, please, it's important.' A faint dawn light was beginning to sift through the big open window. Jeremy looked ghastly. But to be fair, almost anyone at that hour and in that light would look terrible. 'Someone rode Ransom almost to death. When I came in I went back to check on Mouse—to make sure he hadn't been shipped to the butcher again. And coming back I saw Ransom lying in his stall, gasping, his sides bleeding, dried foam around his mouth. There was nobody in the stable or the house—no one. I found you up here and tried to wake you up. I really did. I yelled and shook you as hard as I could. But you were out cold. So then I had to try the vet myself.'

I told Jeremy the rest of what happened, what Dr Reynolds said, about the arrival of Matthew and Dr Mortimer, and what Penelope said when she came home.

'That's why I have to know who did that to Ransom. Not just for Ransom's sake. But for John's. This is a dreadful thing to have happened in his stable.'

In the dim light I hadn't really looked carefully at Jeremy's face as I talked, but I did then, and to my consternation, saw tears coursing down his cheeks in two dirty tracks. 'Jeremy,' I said and put my hand over his.

'She's a terrible woman, Perdita. She's trying to ruin John—both his stable and his name. And I know she's not alone. I don't know about the bills for sure, but I had a suspicion. People'd make remarks when I passed. I was afraid to ask. Because if I found out, then I'd have to do something about it. I've been with the Stantons since I was a boy. I couldn't know what was wrong and not do something. So, because I'm a drunk and a coward, I tried not to know. Because you see, she told me once, when I tried to interfere over something, that she could tell everyone what a drunk I was. That I wasn't reliable with the horses. And I'd never get a job with the horses for the rest of my life. And they've been my life. Only drink have I liked better. And so I haven't done right by them, either....' And the tears came down his cheeks again.

I was thinking hard. 'When did Estes leave?' I asked.

He shook his head. 'I don't know. I remember him bringing me that special Irish whiskey, and taking the first long swallow of it. And him sittin' there smilin'.... He said he had to go home right away.'

'But you don't *remember* him going home.'

'No—God help me, I don't.'

'Ransom's been badly ridden before. I know. In fact, I hid Ransom from Estes—but you know that, Jeremy, you told me where to hide him. Did you know Estes was so enraged when I wouldn't tell him where Ransom was that he brought his crop down on Graymalkin and raised a terrible welt? And he would have done it again if John hadn't stopped him.' And I told him an edited version of what happened.

'He's a bitter, violent fellow when he's crossed. But maybe it was your hiding Ransom that set off his rage. Made him certain he was going to teach Ransom a lesson. That's all he cares about in horses—just so he can show how powerful he is in controlling them. He's an evil man. And when he has the drink or some other

228

rotten sauce in him, then he's like the devil himself.'

'What other rotten sauce?'

Jeremy shrugged. 'Drugs. They're a fast-living set he belongs in. Those after-the-hunt parties can be as racy as all get-out—some of them. As much as what we're told goes on in New York or California. Drink was always my friend—I hated the other stuff. But the people in the country now are up to as much fun and games as the city folk are. And that kind of thing can take a man many ways—just as liquor can.'

'But would Penelope wink at it? It's her stable, too.'

'Ay, it's a puzzlement, that. You'd think she'd be careful of her own reputation. But I think she has other fish to fry. But if you quote me, Perdita, I'll have no place to go.'

'I won't quote you, Jeremy. I promise.'

I was downstairs early, somewhat the worse for having been without a night's sleep, but more or less functioning, when Penelope walked down the corridor, to where I was cleaning out Graymalkin's stall.

'I want to talk to you,' she said.

'Here I am,' I replied, dumping a large forkful onto the wheelbarrow outside.

'No—in my office. Please come right away.' And without waiting for my assent, she walked off.

I did a few more forkfuls, just to keep up my end of things, then patted Graymalkin and followed Penelope's back into the house.

'All right,' she said, sitting down at her desk. She waved at a straight chair a few feet away. 'You can sit down if you want.'

Thank you so kindly, I said mentally, and sat down in the seat she indicated.

'What is it you want me for?' I asked, crossing one knee, and trying to look casual.

'I want you to concentrate on training Nancy for the Burwell show. You saw how well she did in the Maiden Equitation class. You didn't believe me then, and I was right. Well, I'm right now. I want her to compete in the Novice class at the Burwell, and I want her to do well.'

'Penelope,' I said, 'Nancy has just arrived at the point where she enjoys riding and likes her horse. Let her get to where she wants to go into the next class by herself. Then her chances of doing well will be much greater.'

I might as well have not spoken.

'You can start this morning.'

I resent being run over as though I were an obstacle in the road. 'And while we're talking,' I said. 'What about Ransom? Somebody—and

I strongly suspect it's Estes Conrad—nearly killed that horse last night.'

'You leave Estes to me.'

'If he gets into another mood like that, he'll kill Ransom, and I'm not going to hang around waiting for that to happen.'

She looked up, then. It's not easy to describe the expression in her eyes. But I found myself thinking that people who killed in cold blood must look like that.

'You'll do just as I say, Perdita. I know all about your lost memory. If you have such an inability to recall things—how do I know that you didn't reduce Ransom to that condition? No matter how much you might deny it, you might just have forgotten, mightn't you?'

'I was with Matthew until a few moments before I found Ransom,' I said.

'True. But, as you have pointed out, that's not the only time Ransom has been in poor condition. And Jeremy, Jeremy the drunk, is not so reliable as to be above suspicion. Estes is known to have a quick temper. But I think, in this area, his reputation would stand against yours, or Jeremy's or John's.'

'Matthew Shaw would certainly confirm everything I said about yesterday evening.'

She smiled. 'We'll see. But there's no reason even to think in those terms. You train Nancy

231

to do well in the Burwell—and no one will have to confirm anything, will they?'

'You're a blackmailer, Penelope. You're trying to blackmail me just as you have John and Jeremy. You can shout to the whole world about my lost memory—in fact, at this point you might be doing me a favour. Maybe someone who knows me will hear and will come forward and identify me.' I was bluffing and the trouble was, Penelope knew it. Why I still most ardently did not want the world to know about my lost memory, I didn't understand. But everything in me rose against making the information public.

'You don't have the right face for bluffing, Perdita. It shows. Please do as I say, and we'll forget about this conversation.'

But I was determined to get something out of the encounter, even if I had to knuckle under. 'It's true you could make all kinds of accusations that could make life difficult for me right now. But so can I, about you. And I want your word that Estes Conrad will not be let near Ransom. It's no use your saying you can't stop him, because I know you can. And if he ever so much as comes near Ransom—let alone ride and abuse him—I'll talk loud and clear to the humane society. And no matter what you say there'll be people who believe me. For one thing—it's a lot easier for somebody Estes' size to make a mess of a horse like that, than for me—no matter how good a rider I am. So just remember that.' And I walked out.

I felt better having flung down that gauntlet, but I was far from reassured about Ransom. No matter what I said, I wasn't at all sure that if Estes got drunk and violent again, he could be stopped by Penelope—or anyone else. And for John to try something, with Penelope's threat hanging over his head, might be a calamity.

I was brooding about this on my way back to Graymalkin's stall when I came across John in the grooming area, helping to ready the new big black horse for travel. Just outside the courtyard gate I could see the horse trailer drawn up and open.

'You're sending him back,' I said, pleased.

'Yes.' He put down the brush and ran his hands over the horse's coat, his back to me.

I waited for him to turn around, but he didn't. 'John,' I said, 'could I talk to you for a minute or so after you've sent the horse off?'

'I'm busy this afternoon.'

I was beginning to get irritated. 'Come on, John. You know we have to talk.' There were several men standing around, including Jeremy and Lucian. But I was indifferent to them.

He turned around then, his eyes the colour of a leaden sky. 'You don't take hints, do you? We have nothing to discuss. You are Penelope's employee, and I would be grateful if you would do the work you were hired to do and stop following me around and bothering me.' He turned back. 'Jeremy? Let's get this horse into the van.'

In the preceding eight or nine months, I had learned enough about myself to know that I had a quick temper. I hadn't had occasion to realize that I could go completely numb. It was as though I had received a stunning blow across the face that had wiped out all feeling. I heard a slight snigger behind me. I turned. Lucian ducked into the tack room. No one else was looking at me. One man had turned and was examining the notices on the bulletin board in the grooming area. The others were out surrounding the horse, which was being led through the gate.

I turned and went to Graymalkin's stall and in a daze, finished grooming him. Then I went to Mouse's, passing Ransom's stall on the way. The big horse was up and was munching a bran mash. He looked better than he had the night before. But he certainly didn't look his usual vital self. His coat was dull, and there was a listless quality about him. I started to open the stall door, and discovered it was locked. If I had been convinced that it was solely to keep out Estes Conrad, I would have felt better. But I also felt that it might have been locked to keep me out.

'The mistress says nobody's to go in except her and myself,' Jeremy said, coming up behind me.

'What about Estes Conrad?' I asked.

Jeremy shrugged. 'You do what you can do. And if that's all you can do, then that's all. Leave it be, missy. Leave it be. He'll be all right.'

'I wish I could believe you.'

For a half minute I almost succumbed to asking Jeremy what on earth could have gotten into John. But I didn't. What had gotten into John was all too obvious: a strong desire to unload me. Plainly he bitterly regretted that moment of tenderness the night before.

I was finishing grooming Mouse when Nancy turned up in her riding outfit. 'Mummy says I'm to have a two-hour lesson now.' She was back to looking the way she did before the previous horse show—frightened and rather rigid.

'Do you want to do this, Nancy? Try for the Novice class in a stiffer horse show?'

'Oh yes. I *must*. I want to. Please teach me,

235

Perdita. If you don't...please!'

I'd have given much at that moment to collect my bag and leave the stable for good, with or without paycheque. I now understood why the atmosphere at Stanton had struck me right at the beginning as depressed. It was more than depressed. There was an element of sheer malevolence there that was frightening. I glanced at Nancy's face. What would her mother do to her if I didn't train her? If she couldn't compete in the Burwell Novice class, or, if she did, and made a fool of herself, what would happen to her? A more self-reliant child would simply take off. A more defiant one would have fought back.... But there was nothing about Nancy that gave me any confidence that she could bring herself to do that. All I could do, at this moment, was play for time.

'Okay. Start getting Bayou ready. I'll go up and change and be ready in a minute.'

'Why do you have to change? You've ridden in jeans and chaps before.'

'Because my other jeans are more comfortable. It's easier to ride in them.'

'But I've never saddled Bayou before.'

'Then it's high time you started. Besides, it's not that hard. You've seen it done. And you love Bayou, don't you?'

236

Her face relaxed. 'Yes.'

'All right then.'

Upstairs I took off my jeans, threw them in the bathtub with some detergent, and took the others out of the closet. After I'd zipped them up, I automatically put my hands in the pockets to make sure I had a few dollars and a tissue. Both were there, and so was a hard piece of cardboard. I took it out. 'Agatha Mitchell, Fairacre Farm.' And I saw again the woman with the pleasant voice, the straight blue eyes, and the roughened hands. Staring at the card, an idea formed in my mind. 'Possible, possible,' I muttered to myself, and went down the stairs to join Nancy.

The numbness, the sense of having been brutally and publicly chastised, stayed with me throughout the day, as I schooled Nancy over jump after jump, and made her trot, canter, walk, change lead step, and ride with and without stirrups. I would have welcomed rage, which would have at least have fuelled my ability to make some kind of response—to shove John's arrogant words back in his face and humiliate him as he had humiliated me. Finally, towards the end of the day, some sense of my own anger made itself felt. But it was not the kind of anger that produced energy and action. All it yielded was an overwhelming desire to flee and never come back.

But first I had to do something about Mouse and Ransom.

On my next afternoon off I caught the bus at the end of the road and had myself put down within a mile of Fairacre Farm. When I got there, the farm turned out to be a pleasant, rather higgledy-piggledy place, with the stables built in a variety of sheds and outbuildings, plus an old-fashioned barn.

'I'd like to speak to Mrs Mitchell,' I said, to the first stable hand that passed.

'Well, as of this morning, you're out of luck. She left for the Coast late last night, and won't be back for a month. Anything I can do?'

If I'd just discovered that card a day sooner! But a day sooner and I would have still cherished the illusion that John Stanton and I were on the same side. Now I knew it was not true. He might care about paying his bills—after all, that was his business. But I was pretty sure by now that he didn't care for the welfare of the horse apart from its property value. 'Would you be willing to board a couple of horses for me?' I asked, wondering where I was going to get the money if he agreed. I had a feeling that if I told Mrs Mitchell at least part of the truth— that the two horses, Mouse and Ransom—were in some kind of danger, I could have worked out a financial arrangement with her. Well, I'd find the money somewhere.

But he shook his head. 'We can't do that until she comes back. We don't have too many empty stalls, and one of the things she's gone to California for is to get some new stock. You'll have to wait until she comes back.'

'All right.' I turned away.

Perhaps something of what I was feeling conveyed itself to the man. 'Who shall I say asked, if she calls back?'

'I don't think my name would mean much. It's Perdita Smith. Tell her I was the girl she met on the road when my...when my horse took off.'

'Okay.'

Matthew had called when I returned, and I returned his call. He would not have been my choice as a person to turn to, but my options at this point were severely limited.

'Hi,' he said, when he came to the phone. 'I was wondering if you could make dinner next Wednesday.'

I had arrived at the stage where I didn't much like to leave the stable, unless it was necessary. I was not sure what I would find— or not find—when I got back. But I wanted to ask a favour of Matthew, so I accepted.

'I'll meet you down at the end of the drive as I did before,' I said.

'I can come and pick you up at the house if you like,' he said casually. 'I'll have the smaller car.'

But I didn't want everyone at Stanton to know that I was having dinner with Matthew, although I wasn't sure why I felt that way. 'Oh, I don't mind. I'd just as soon walk out the drive.'

'Okay. Seven?'

'Fine.'

Ever since the episode in the courtyard, John and I had been avoiding one another. And when we did meet, we each pretended the other wasn't there. Ludicrous as it could have been, it was not too hard. I went into the house only for meals, and John was almost never there at that time. What he did about eating I didn't know and didn't care. The atmosphere around the farm, never cheery, became increasingly tense. Jeremy shook a lot, which I took as an indication of his attempted abstemiousness. The door to Ransom's stall remained locked, but that did not prevent me from giving him a carrot whenever no one was looking.

But one time someone was looking.

'You're an idiot to do that,' Lucian said, passing rapidly behind me with a feed sack.

'I suppose you'll go rushing off to your mother to tell her of my infraction of the law.'

He put the feed sack down. 'I'm a lot of things. But I'm not—usually—a sneak. Not unless it's my neck or else.'

'So she has something over you, too,' I said, not really thinking he'd answer me. But he did.

'Oh sure. That's the only way Mom knows how to operate—find something on somebody and then you have them.'

I was in so much agreement with what he said that it took me a minute to take in something else: that that was a singularly terrible thing to say about one's parent—let alone think it.

'It's too bad she's like that,' I said. 'Too bad for everybody, and I suppose for her, although I can't work up much sympathy.'

'You and everybody else.'

I was tempted to ask what she had hanging over him, but decided that since it was obviously not my business, he'd probably tell me to butt out. To my surprise, he offered the information.

'One night a friend and I were here—not an upper-class type from one of the stables, just a guy from the village. We were sharing a joint and got careless. The place started to burn—'

'My God!' I said. To anyone who loves

241

horses even the suggestion of a barn fire is horrifying. 'Did...did any of the horses get burned?'

'No. But the fire department was sent for, and they nosed around and found the joint, and started asking questions. Mom gave the guy I was with a lot of money to say he was smoking while waiting for me to finish with the barn chores and then to split out of town and go somewhere they couldn't put their hands on him.'

'And supposing they found out that you'd been smoking, too. It's not a hanging offence. Anyway, it was an accident.'

Lucian leaned against the stall. 'Mom said that they'd find out pretty quick that I was also—' he hesitated, then went on, 'er, sometimes...selling grass, plus a couple of other things.'

'Why?' I asked, surprised. 'Was it for the money, or just general cussedness?'

He shrugged. 'Both, I guess. She keeps me here by threatening to tell the police and/or my father about my attempts at private enterprise. Because of that, and because she has other things she wants to do with her money— like buy expensive horses and push Nancy into the hunt set—she just doles out nickels and dimes, at least to me. I guess she also figures that if she gives me enough money I'll split and get on a bus.'

'Where to?'

He looked at me a minute before answering. 'Arizona. That's where my old man is.'

'Do you like him?'

'Yeah. He's okay.' Lucian picked up a strand of hay and chewed it a minute. 'He's a wrangler. Takes horses from ranch to ranch. Also has a small place of his own.'

Somehow I was surprised. 'But you don't like horses.'

'Well—those horses work. They're not being fed and pampered while I don't have enough money to get into town.'

'It's not horses you don't like. It's being here.'

'You can say that again.'

'How did your mother find out about your drug dealing?'

'The way she finds everything out. She listened once on the phone when I was talking to Tony—that's the guy I was smoking with. He wanted to get some grass from me and knew I had some.' Lucian threw away the strand of hay and kicked the feed sack. 'That's how she got to know about you—listening to your conversation with that nun. She's quite a listener!'

I remembered the click on the phone when

I was talking to Reverend Mother.

'Why are you telling me this?'

He shrugged. 'What's the difference? Even if you told about her, Mom has everything so set up that the only person who'd look bad is you—sour grapes because you were fired, or something. She's good at that.'

'Just as a matter of curiosity,' I said, 'how do you feel about your mother?'

He looked up for a minute. 'I hate her guts,' he said. 'And so does Nancy, poor shrimp! Only she hasn't got the moxie to do anything about it. And there's even talk—but that's enough gossip for one day.' He gave a sour grin.

'What does she have over John?' I heard myself ask, though I'd sworn an oath that I would not, by thought, word or deed, show the slightest interest in him.

'I dunno—she doesn't confide in me. One night old Jeremy got drunk and told me it was something to do with a stable boy that used to work here and that John was supposed to have half-killed. He's a fast man with his fists.'

I knew the moment he said it that it was probably true. I detested John Stanton with every fibre of my being, but nothing could make me really visualize him chiselling or embezzling, crimes that theoretically she might be holding

244

over his head. But half-killing somebody who didn't jump fast enough when he said jump—I had no trouble at all in believing that.

'I have a favour to ask you,' I said to Matthew over dinner. We were at a smaller, quieter place that I liked a lot better than the previous one.

'You've got it,' Matthew said, and reached over to put his hand over mine. I wished that I liked having it there better, and repressed the impulse to pull it away. The favour I had to ask involved the safety of both Mouse and Ransom, so I concentrated on them and left my hand where it was.

'Would you let me board two horses at Devereux—at least for a short while, until I can make other arrangements?'

'Sure.' He stared at me a moment. 'What's the story?—there has to be one since you've plenty of room at Stanton.'

'I'd rather not go into it if you don't mind. One horse, Mouse, is mine, and I can board him where I want....' What had started out as an explanatory statement to give some reason why I was appealing to Matthew was, I saw in a minute, a grave mistake. If I had just stuck with my original intention, which was simply to ask to board the horses, I would have been far better off. People could speculate all they wanted, but I wouldn't have told them anything. Now, not only was I making it obvious that I wouldn't—or couldn't—board my horses at Stanton, I had also just revealed that one of the horses didn't even belong to me. Congratulations, Perdita, I thought sarcastically.

'And the other horse—the one I assume is *not* yours?'

I had to go all the way, now. I looked straight at Matthew. 'Estes Conrad got drunk one night and half killed the horse. I want to get him out of there before he does it again.'

'It's pretty odd that everyone at Stanton doesn't want the same. Why don't they report him to the humane society?'

'I don't know. I don't think Penelope cares about anything but her rising social status. And I think she'd forgive Estes Conrad a lot more than a beaten horse.'

'And John?'

No matter what he'd done, I couldn't betray him. 'He's been away.'

'I see.'

'Okay, I'll get the horses and take them to Devereux, and enter them under fictitious names. Nobody has to know they came from Stanton—at least for a while. And I'll hide 'em in one of the back barns.'

'Nobody'd think twice about old Mouse, but wouldn't somebody think it funny about Ransom—he's a pretty good horse, at least when he's okay he is.'

'I can talk about an eccentric Arab owner, afraid one of his brother's rival tribesmen might do him in, or something.'

I grinned. 'Well, I won't quibble. The next problem is, how much does it cost?'

'A lot. Devereux's not cheap. Now if you were just working there, you could keep them there in exchange for some of your salary.'

This had occurred to me. And although I found myself as little attracted by the idea of working at Devereux (or leaving Stanton?) as ever, it was about the only way I could manage keeping the horses there. 'Okay,' I said. 'I accept.'

For a second there was an expression in his eyes that seemed strange, and then it was gone before I could define it.

'Wonderful,' he said. 'How soon can you come?'

'I don't know. I'll have to see.' Having made the decision I knew I had to make, I discovered I felt worse, not better.

'And there's another little matter. What you are planning to do, according to what you tell me, is no less than to steal a horse. One, you tell me, belongs to you. But the other—a valuable horse according to what you say—is the property of Estes Conrad. When everything hits the fan—as it's going to do, sooner or later—how are you going to justify it? I only ask because I'm going to need a cover story, too. I can say I didn't know, but I don't know how far that'll fly. The penalties for stealing valuable horses can be pretty steep.'

That problem had, of course, occurred to me, too. 'I don't know.'

'Never mind. We'll think of something. The main thing is to put the horse where Conrad can't get at it. And the sooner the better, I should think.'

As always, I checked on Mouse when I got back. He was happy to see me in a sleepy way. And quite grateful for his carrot. Then I turned down another hall and went to Ransom's stall. Both the upper and lower doors were open. And the stall was empty.

CHAPTER TEN

I stood there for a long time, staring at the empty stall, wondering what I could or should do. Then I went to the tack room where his saddle and tack were kept on nails over his name. They were gone. My heart sank. The move, wherever it was to, looked permanent.

Finally there was nothing to do but go to bed, where I lay awake stroking Cassandra, thinking of everything that might have happened to Ransom: Estes Conrad could have taken him away and boarded him elsewhere—the most likely, and also the most frightening. He could have been sold—but who would want to sell him when he was less than his best? Penelope could have sent him somewhere else. I knew that was untrue before the thought was formulated. Why should she—unless to spike any gossip that might have got out about Ransom's condition. Jeremy? Possibly. John? Trying to analyze John's possible motives made me miserable, no matter what attitude I took. If I thought he had sent the horse away for its own safety, then it would be to his credit, but of course that made me feel even worse about his treatment of me—his insulting rejection and public slap in the face. If I thought he allowed Estes to move the horse, then obviously his profit meant more to him than the health and safety of that magnificent animal.... The more I considered what he had allowed to go on, the more I leaned to the latter explanation. And after all, wasn't he paying tribute to Penelope's blackmail? Better that the horses be injured than that he be exposed.... Having satisfied myself about the truth of this, I went to sleep wondering why I was more miserable than ever.

The next morning I said to Jeremy, 'What happened to Ransom?'

The old man looked at me over the tack he was polishing. 'He's been put away—put down—for his own good. He got took sick in the night. It's best that way.'

All I could see within my mind was that terrible place where I'd found Mouse, with its dreadful smell of death. 'You can't mean it, Jeremy. You can't. You're telling me that horrible woman sent him to that butcher's place?'

'Ach, no. Not Ransom. The Dead Arrival Service was sent for and he was put down here, and the van then came to take his body. And it's no use going on like that. It was done while you weren't here because you'd just take on about it, and John's had enough of that, thank you very much. Now just give over. Have done. He's gone. Forget him!'

'I'll never forget him. Never. Never!' All I could think about was that magnificient chestnut, with his fine spirit and his good heart—if he had just been treated halfway decently. Turning on my heel I went to Mouse's stall, groomed and saddled him and took him out. I rode for a long time, numb with anger and pity. People who used animals for their own good with no regard to the animals as living, sensate beings, with as much right to be in the universe as humans, made me sick at the stomach and wild with rage.

After cantering for a long time down the trails, I realized that Mouse had had enough, and slowed to a trot and then a walk. After I thought he'd cooled I got off, took off his bridle and let him nuzzle grass for a while, while I lay on my back and stared at the blue sky and the round puff balls of clouds.

How long I'd been doing that I didn't know, but eventually two realizations made themselves to the top of my mind. One was that other than mourn him, there was nothing I could do about Ransom. The other was that I was leaving Stanton as soon as I could get back, call Matthew, and arrange to have Mouse picked up. If Penelope wanted to broadcast my mental problems, then let her.

I returned slowly, hours after I should have been teaching Nancy, fully determined on my course. There would be nothing that Penelope could say or threaten to stop me. And as for John, I knew he had gone off to a horse auction in another state and would not be back until the day of the Burwell.

But I had not counted on Nancy herself.

'You can't leave a week before the Burwell, Perdita. You just can't! You know how Mummy is. She'll make me go through the class anyway. And if I do badly—and I will—I don't know what she'll do to me. Yes, I do, she'll kill me!'

'Don't be silly, Nancy!' I said. 'That's idiotic! She'll probably be cross and unpleasant—but beside that, what can she do?' Which was a brainless thing to say, since I, above any outsider, should have known what Penelope could do when she wanted something. She didn't hesitate to blackmail her son; why would I think she'd be tender-minded about her daughter?

'*Please!*'

If Nancy had cried or wrung her hands or pulled any of the classic tricks usually used to elicit sympathy, I might have been able to hold out. But when I glanced over and saw her standing there in the entrance to the grooming room where I was unsaddling Mouse, a desperate, terrified look on her face, I gave in.

'Okay. All right. You win. But I'm going to work your tail off and I don't want to hear any more whimperings about your not wanting to do it.'

'I won't, I won't! Oh, Perdita—thank you!' And a little to my embarrassment she ran over and flung her arms around me. 'I'll go get Bayou ready!'

I pondered giving notice anyway, telling Penelope I'd leave the day after the Burwell. But who knew what petty revenge that monster woman would take while I was still at Stanton? I never felt entirely safe about Mouse, and I certainly felt even less so now, with Ransom destroyed. I would therefore bottle my feelings and not give Perdita any flank or surface to attack while I was still on the premises.

The only thing I was able to do was stay out of Penelope's and John's way. That, since John was away the entire time, and Penelope part of the time, offered no problem. Even Lucian didn't seem to be around much, although I

253

caught occasional glimpses of him as he went doggedly about his tasks of mucking out the stalls, cleaning the tack, and letting many of the horses out into the fields when their owners couldn't exercise them. Whether or not he regretted having told me what he did I couldn't be sure, but he seemed to steer clear of me.

Even Jeremy muttered sourly one day that Penelope, eager for me to have as much time to instruct Nancy as possible, had told him to help me out in my other chores. So Nancy and I spent a large part of each day for the remaining week down at the ring or out on the trail while I schooled and drilled and instructed and encouraged until I felt the horses themselves would rebel at the sound of my voice.

'For God's sake, Nancy. Use more leg. That's your main aid in conveying to the horse what you want him to do. By now you know when and how to do it, so *do* it.... Don't burst over the jump like that. Get ready for it earlier .... And don't rush it.... I've told you before, let him have a controlled canter, but the operative word is *control—you* control.... No, don't hang on your reins like that—you know better than that...and think of Bayou's feelings....' And so on. An appeal to Nancy to consider Bayou's sensibilities always worked. She had become devoted to the patient horse, and the

254

two of them worked well together. She was still not entirely at ease on another horse, which was natural, but I was reasonably sure that would come.... She should, I thought, given moderate luck and the right circumstances, at least do respectably.

But the right circumstances were more problematical at the Burwell than at the smaller show of a few weeks back. The Burwell was a top local show, attracting the finest riders in the area, and there would be, at that show, I was reasonably sure, the kind of tension that is found wherever the elite of any profession gather. Novices and newcomers would show proper awe and try to keep out of the way when giants and experts came to display their skills with the casual cachet that appeared to the neophyte as godlike. And how did I know all that...?

Because I remembered it. I had been to such shows. I could rebuild them from my returning memory, most of the images coming back, ready to be summoned.

This was the world I'd grown up in. I realized that now. I could retrieve individual faces, but not always the names that went with them; scenes, although I wasn't sure how well I knew the players. The great horse shows are similiar in many respects. The rings are much the same, the jumps placed in the same way. Schooling areas—the areas or runs where contestants are given final coaching by their instructors—were located in different parts of the grounds, depending on size and shape, but they, too, were mostly alike.

I also knew, although I wasn't sure how I knew, that I had been to the Burwell before. I could not remember the environment, or how the rings were placed, or the names of the individuals concerned with it. But I knew I had been there.

Strangely, the effect knowing this had on me was to fill me with unease about going. The nearer the day got, the more I wished there were some way Nancy could go with her mother, or even John, and be able to function there as well as though I were with her. Most of the time I knew this was impossible: her mother made her nervous and frightened and John terrorized her. Even her schooling went better on the days when Penelope was absent. Once, when Penelope was on a business trip for two or three days and Nancy had excelled in the ring accordingly, I said, as we were riding back to the barn, 'Nancy, I wish you would go to the Burwell by yourself. There's no reason you shouldn't do quite well without me, and you'll certainly have other members of Stanton there.'

It was the wrong thing to say, of course, as I should have known it would be.

'Oh, Perdita—please don't say that. Don't even *suggest* that you mightn't be there. If you don't go, I won't either, and Mother will kill me. If you're not there I'll mess up in some way, and Mother will kill me over that.' And her voice started the quiver that meant that in thirty seconds or less, she'd start to cry.

'All right, I'll be there, I promise. Good heavens, Nancy! Someday you're going to have to confront your mother, or, if you don't, you'll never have any peace....'

My voice faltered and came to a stop. I was overwhelmed with a sense of déjà vu, the disconcerting sensation of living through something I'd experienced before.

'What's the matter, Perdita?'

'Nothing,' I said, which was a lie. I was shaken. Had I said what I'd just finished saying to Nancy to someone at another time? Had someone said it to me? I had no actual memory of the latter, but it felt right, and I recalled now recently remembering my mother's face, but remembering it in an emotional vacuum.

'Well, you look funny.' Nancy's voice seemed to come from far off.

I glanced at the child and read genuine

concern. Yes, she needed to have me healthy and functioning for her big contest, but I saw in her eyes affection also. After all, I thought, whose motives are always unmixed?...Certainly not mine.

On an impulse, I said, 'Nancy, there's something about me you don't know, which would explain moments when you find me—well, strange, or puzzling.' And I told her about my lost memory. 'The trouble is,' I went on, 'by now it's not entirely lost. There are large areas I remember, although I can't always remember the people, or if I remember them I don't always recall their names, or their connection to me, or how I felt about them. I think that's what bothers me...I can't remember how I *felt*. And that's why I said what I did about the Burwell. I have the strongest feeling I've been there before, but I can't remember the circumstances or who I was with. And I suppose I'm afraid that if I go back—because it's the only circumstance, or event, in my past that I *know* I was at—then everything will come rushing back....'

'Don't you want it to?'

I looked at the child, and it seemed to me that she showed a maturity she hadn't been credited with by me or anyone else. I made a face. 'You have a point. Of course I do, theoretically. You talk about being afraid of your mother—afraid of confronting her. Well, evidently I'm afraid of finding something out about myself—although I don't know what it is. Crazy, isn't it?' And I started to laugh. After a minute she giggled too.

'Well, we're both scared, I guess,' she said. 'Maybe it's not so bad, anyway, not as bad as being scared all by yourself.'

I grinned. 'True.'

That evening Matthew phoned. I hadn't talked to him, so he didn't know about Ransom's death.

'Then I think it's even more important for you to come here,' he said when I told him. 'That's too crazy a place for you to be.'

'I think so too,' I was unable or unwilling to go into my lack of enthusiasm for going to Devereux. 'But I can't leave before the Burwell. Nancy's competing there, and since I'm instructing her, it would be desertion of the worst kind. I'll come to work after that.'

There was a silence. 'Well, we really need you before. There are some beginners here who badly want coaching before they go into the ring at the Burwell. If you don't come, An—Ann is going to have to hire an instructor, and your chances of getting the job then, after the show, drop by about ninety percent.'

'You didn't tell me that,' I said.

'Sorry, I thought I made it clear.'

'Would I have to go to the Burwell?' I said slowly.

'Don't you want to?'

'No. No, I don't.'

'Why not?'

I almost told him, as I had told Nancy. But something stopped me. Instead I said, 'I loathe those big shows. I really do. One of the reasons I'm tempted not to stay here is that I would have to go with Nancy.'

'Well then for God's sake pick your horse up and come over here now. You don't have to go anywhere near the show. There are plenty of instructors going. They can take over the beginners at the show itself.'

It was humiliating how much I wanted to forget my promise to Nancy. How much I wanted *not* to go to the Burwell. But as I glanced out the open grooming area to Nancy, combing Bayou's tail, I knew I couldn't do it.

'I'm sorry, Matthew. I'd like to accept, I really would. More than I can say. But I can't. I can't let the child down now—not with her mother being the way she is. I'll just have to trust that you're able to hold that job for me.'

'I think you're crazy,' Matthew said with sudden anger.

'No, I'm not crazy. My memory may be faulty—although I'm glad to say it seems to be coming back in large hunks. But I'm not crazy. If you think that we're not on the same wavelength, wouldn't you feel that way towards somebody who depended on you?'

'Sure. Sorry, I didn't mean that. It's just—oh well, don't be mad. I'll see you at the show on Wednesday. That's the day you're going.'

'Yes. Maybe another day, too. But I don't know yet.'

'How about dinner tonight?'

'No, I can't. There's something else I have to do.'

'Another guy,' sounding so genuinely let down that I laughed. 'No.' And then, because it sounded so wild, 'Would you believe a nun?'

'You've got to be kidding! You're not taking the veil?'

'No, no, no! Why do people always say that? She's just a friend. I...I stayed with her once.'

'Where?'

'St John's Convent. The sanitarium on Route Twenty-two.'

'Oh yes. When were you there?'

'That's a long story.'

'But you won't tell me tonight?'

'No. Soon—but not tonight.'

He gave a theatrical sigh. 'Okay. I accept my fate. But reluctantly, you understand.'

I laughed and hung up. But just before I did, I heard a click. So Penelope was up to her old tricks. Well, let her, I thought! She didn't scare me any more because I had nothing to hide.

My mind and emotions were such an ill-assorted collection of thoughts and feelings that I hoped an hour of Mother Julian's brisk common sense would bring some order to them. And, along with the general muddle, was a curious conviction nagging me as I drove, that I had just made a mistake about something. But every time I almost knew what it was, the whole thing slipped away. 'The hell with it,' I said aloud, finally, in exasperation, as I turned in the convent gates.

I was right that an hour with Mother Julian made me feel better, but it was more because she stiffened my spine than brought order to my jumbled head.

'Well,' she said somewhat indignantly, when I explained my fears about the Burwell. 'Isn't that what we've all been striving for for the past months? To restore what you've lost—your memory?'

'Then why do I dread it so much?'

'I don't know. That's probably one of the things you'll find out. But running away is not going to help.'

'I was afraid you'd say that,' I said.

'You knew I would. That's why you came. You'll just have to face it.'

Again there flashed that sense of déjà vu. *I have been here before, this has happened before....* 'I have a feeling what you've just said was said to me before, that somebody said it to me before.... It happened when I said the same to Nancy about her mother, you know, as I just told you.'

Mother Julian nodded. 'Even people without lost memories have that feeling.'

'What does it mean when people who haven't lost their memories have it?'

'There are lots of theories. One is that you've simply forgotten something that occurred, or it could have happened in early childhood and been buried. Other people—people who believe in reincarnation—believe that it's a flash from a previous life.'

'Do you believe that?'

'Let's say I don't disbelieve it.'

'Can Christians believe it?'

'Lots do. But that's not what we're talking about. I don't think you're getting glimpses from a previous life. I think you're getting glimpses of your own life, some of which is cut off.'

'Well, all of it was cut off, but a lot of it is back. Only not the feelings.'

'They'll probably return when the rest of your memory does. And when that happens...' She paused, then leaned over and grasped my hands. 'I want you to think about something that the fourteenth-century mystic, Julian of Norwich, whose name I took when I came into the order, said. "All shall be well and all shall be well, and all manner of things shall be well." Hang onto that for dear life. And call me.'

It was on my way back that I had the accident. I had borrowed Jeremy's runabout, and had discovered that, like Jeremy himself, it was not in the best of condition. However, it got me there and was getting me back when I crossed the main highway. Perhaps my attention was not all it might have been: the feeling of having missed something important had returned to nag me after I had left the convent grounds. Consequently, I almost missed the stop sign as the road arrived at the intersection with the highway. But I stopped and looked both ways; evidently, though, not carefully enough, nor with my full attention. Because when I started up again and began crossing the highway, a car came out of nowhere, or, more accurately, from behind trees bordering the road at my left. One minute there was a blank road, the next minute a fearsome noise and the sight of a much bigger car bearing down on the left. I reacted instinctively, stamping on the accelerator. The oncoming car hit the back of mine with a terrible bang and crunch, swinging it almost around back to front, then sped on into the night. My car swerved, tottered for a moment, then slid backwards into the ditch at the side of the road.

By some miracle I seemed to be in one piece, although I felt sick and was shaking all over. A seat belt had prevented me from being flung either onto the side window or the windshield, so my head hadn't hit, but I still felt dizzy.

Somehow my fumbling hand found the ignition and I turned the key, although I was afraid the back wheels were too deeply embedded in the ditch for the car to be able to get out on its own strength. The motor turned and died. I waited a moment and tried again. The response was even briefer. For what felt like a long time I tried to get the engine started, but it seemed dead beyond recall.

Finally I gave up and began the delicate business of trying to get myself out. The car's rear was not only in the ditch, the body of the car was half keeled over. Should I follow gravity and get out the passenger side, or should I try to climb up and out my side? Eventually I did that and emerged, shaking and bruised, at the side of the road. Beside me the front of the car aimed at the sky like a derelict building. Still badly shaken by the crash, it took me a minute to get my bearings. Then I saw, at the back of me, the road I had been intending to take when the other car hit me. There was nothing to do but walk back along it to the farm, a matter of several miles, and hope to pass a phone booth from which I could call Jeremy to come with one of the farm cars and pick me up. Jeremy, I thought, with a fearful pang of guilt. I had borrowed his car and now it was destroyed.

'Oh God!' I said aloud, and realized that a car had pulled up beside me. In front were a couple, the man driving, and behind were two children.

'Are you all right?' the man said.

I nodded. 'Yes.'

'What happened?'

I told him about being hit.

'And they didn't stop?'

'No.'

'Did you get the license number?'

I shook my head.

'Well, it's amazing what creeps are allowed to drive on our roads. I'm afraid that's the

266

end of your car.'

'And it isn't even mine,' I said.

'That makes it worse, I guess.' He hesitated. 'Can we take you somewhere?'

'Could you ...could you take me to Stanton Farm? That's where I live. It's about twenty minutes in that direction.' And I waved in the direction I was going.

'Of course. But shouldn't we take you to a hospital first? Or a police station?'

'No.' I wanted in the worst way to get back to my own room. I'd been around enough doctors and hospitals to last me the rest of my life. And I certainly didn't want to have to cope with police—not at this juncture. 'Thanks, anyway,' I said. 'But if you could take me back to Stanton I'd be terrifically grateful.'

'No problem. Get in the back. Move over, kids. You know that the police are going to find the car and will be in touch with you,' he said as we started off.

I hadn't particularly thought of it, but realized it would be true, of course. Well, I'd have to cope with that then. 'Yes, I know. I'll talk to them when they come. Thanks a lot for the ride.'

For the next twenty minutes I sat squashed next to the two children in the back of the car until it turned into the side road leading to

267

Stanton. The man's wife was about to ask me some questions when her husband said, 'You probably don't feel too much like talking, do you?'

'No,' I replied, grateful.

The wife smiled. 'I understand.'

They really were a nice family, but I couldn't wait to get back to the farm. Finally, they deposited me outside the gate. 'Sure we can't do anything else?'

'No. I can't thank you enough. You've been wonderful.'

'Here's my card, if you should need me.' And he handed me a card which I put into my jeans pocket.

Telling Jeremy about his car had to be done right away. I found him upstairs in his room, watching television.

'Well,' he said, when I knocked on the open door. 'Ye're back?'

'Yes, Jeremy, I smashed your car.'

That certainly got his attention. 'Me car? It's gone? Ye smashed it?'

I nodded, and felt again the beginning of a headache. The second since I had been at Stanton.'

'I'm sorry, Jeremy. I'm so sorry. Someone ran into me, just as I was crossing the highway. I stopped, I truly stopped. And there was nothing in sight. Then when I was about a quarter of the way across, the car just came out of nowhere. It must have been hidden by that bunch of poplars that are on the right as you cross the road. You know. They're sort of bunched there. Anyway, I speeded up—it was the only thing I could do, and he hit my rear—the rear end of your car, spinning so that its rear end was stuck in the ditch at the side of the road, and then just drove off. I tried to start it again, but it was no go. Finally I got out and stood there wondering what to do. Then a car stopped, and this nice family brought me back. Jeremy, I'm sorry. Really I am.'

'For God's sake, girl, couldn't you see the lights coming?'

'No,' I said. There was a queer little silence as I tried to go back in my mind,... I was driving across, there was a noise on the left, and in the faint light from the last of a late sunset, the shape of the car speeding towards me...I could see the black squarish shape in the front of the car, but there were no lights.

'Jeremy, there weren't any lights.'

'Of course, there were. You just don't remember.'

'No. There weren't. Not one.'

We stared at one another. Then, 'Could you see who was in the car?'

'No. Just a head.'

Another silence. 'Of course,' he said. 'It could have been crazy kids. They drive around stoned on grass and I dunno what else. And drunk....'

A shiver went over me.

'Ach,' Jeremy said. 'It was a bunch of wild kids showing off in front of their girls. That's what it'll be. And there's me insurance. Ye're sure you were obeying the law—doing just what you said.'

'Yes.' I should have been able to foresee trouble about this. But—I had hoped for the best and the best hadn't materialized.

'Jeremy, I was driving without a license.'

'You're the crazy one. Why the hell don't you keep your license about you? You have one, don't you?'

'No.' I took a deep breath and explained why I didn't have a license, and why, since I couldn't answer questions, I had not applied for another.

'I always knew there was something funny about you. So that's it. Lost memory. And now you've lost me car.' Getting up he went to the small hall refrigerator and took out a beer.

'You're not going to get drunk, are you, Jeremy?'

'And what's it to you, miss? What's a few

beers compared to driving without a license? Don't talk to me about drinking.' And he went back to watching the television set.

'Would it help get you more insurance if I said I stole the car?' I asked, wishing to be helpful.

'Ye wanna go to jail?'

'No.'

'Then don't talk daft.'

Tired, depressed and full of a queer foreboding, I went to bed.

The police showed up the next morning.

'You leave this to me,' Jeremy said.

I saw him go out to the two men who were standing in the courtyard and watched them as I groomed Mouse in the grooming area. After a few minutes one of the men walked over.

'So you've lost your memory and have been driving without a license?'

'Yes,' I said. 'I'm sorry.'

'Why didn't you come down to county headquarters, explain your problem, and take a test? If you passed we'd have issued you with another one.'

'I guess because I'm stupid. I just didn't think.'

'Well, you're going to have to appear in court. You know that, don't you? Here.' And

271

he handed me an official piece of paper. 'Now, about that accident. Please describe it to me in the closest detail you can.'

I went through the whole thing again.

'You're sure there were no lights.'

'Absolutely certain.'

'Could you see the car at all?'

'No. It was just a black shape coming at me from the left.'

'You never saw anything else of it?'

'No, how could I? It was—' The mind and memory were strange things—as I had every reason to know. In the months in the hospital, being examined by doctors, answering their questions, asking questions of my own, reading, I came to see memory often not as an unbroken line, but more like a bag of confetti, each piece representing a segment that might or might not be where I could reach it. If that was the case, one piece had just slid into my consciousness. As Jeremy's car swung around after the violent impact, its headlight swerved past the side of the other car, and I had an impression of beige streaked by blue, and, at the edge, a piece of a familiar logo.

'Yes?' the policeman said, patiently. 'You remember something?'

'Just beige with a sort of blue streak and the

beginning of a trademark. I think it was a Chevrolet.'

'Well, that's something. Now this blue streak or stripe. Describe it as well as you can.'

'It didn't look like a stripe. More like a smear. But—I'm not sure.'

He took me back over it again—and again. Finally he said, 'Okay. Now about the head. Did you recognize it?'

'No.'

'Is that because you saw it clearly enough to know it was a person you didn't know? Or did you just not see it clearly?'

'I didn't see it clearly.'

'Was it a man or a woman?'

'I couldn't really tell. But I think it was a man.'

'What do you feel in your gut it was?'

'A man.' Out of the corner of my eye I saw Lucian start to come out into the courtyard, see the policeman and duck back into the barn. His retreat before the person of the law was so blatant that his fear of his mother's threat was suddenly vivid.

'Look,' I said to the officer. 'You know it was Jeremy's car I was in—and that it got smashed. Will the fact that I was driving without a license keep the insurance company from paying?'

'Not if he has the right kind of insurance—and I think he does.' He closed his notebook. 'We'll be in touch. And don't drive again till you get a license.'

'I won't.' It would certainly make life difficult, but that couldn't be helped.

When the policeman had gone I went back into the barn to finish grooming Mouse. Lucian was hovering near Mouse's stall. 'What'd he want?' he asked.

'I was driving Jeremy's car last night when somebody smashed into me. To make things worse, I was driving without a license. The cops aren't happy about that.'

'Pigs!' Lucian said, adding a swipe to the reins he was polishing.

'Come on,' I said. 'He wasn't here because I was driving without a license. He was here to try and find out who crashed into me. Anyway, isn't the "pigs" bit passé?'

'Yeah, well, if it wasn't for the cops Mom couldn't hold that drug thing over my head.'

'It's not all the fault of the cruel outer world, you know. You did sell some grass—at least that's what you told me. Do you intend to make a career out of crime?'

He hung the reins on a hook just inside the tack room. 'Nah. Like I said, it was mostly to annoy Mom and make a buck. And it sure backfired. It gave Mom what she wanted, a hook into me, and I didn't get any dough.'

'How much do you need to get to your father's place?'

'I have a few bucks. I figure about a hundred more would do it.'

'I'll lend it to you.'

He stared at me. 'Why?'

Since I'd just thought of it I wasn't sure myself. Then I said, 'I don't like to see people trapped.'

'And what about you? If Mom finds out it'll just add to her list of things she can hold over your head. You don't know her. She'd probably claim you knew all about my drug dealing.'

'How can she? I've only been here a few months.'

'Then she'll find something else.'

'You really do hate her, don't you? Well, I don't think I'm going to be here much longer. I only stayed this long to help Nancy at the Burwell. And with what happened to Ransom I have a couple of things I can hold over her, too. And there's the vet from Devereux who can vouch for it, not to mention Matthew Shaw.'

'He's at Devereux, too, isn't he?'

'Yes. Do you know him?'

'If you mean, have I met him, no.'

'But you know something about him?'

'Only talk.'

'Saying what?'

Lucian shrugged. 'He's supposed to be big buddies with the Devereux woman's playboy boyfriend.'

'Oh—Sonny Somebody.'

'Yeah. He has some kind of magic with women—was married to some terrifically rich horsey type before he met Ann Devereux. Mind you—he knows horses, that part's real. Everybody gives him that. Wins at shows and all that stuff. Anyway, they say your friend Matthew is big pals with him. Maybe he's on the make, too.'

'You're down on everybody, aren't you?' I spoke sharply. Since I was planning to go to Devereux myself, this was not particularly what I wanted to hear. Still, whatever happened, Mouse would be safe. And I'd be away from Penelope. And John? My heart gave a painful lurch. Better that I be away than here, I thought. Whatever I believed—or hoped—he felt for me was obviously not enough to overcome his determination to keep me out of his life. As for what Matthew was—and some instinct told me that Lucian might not be far wrong about him—well, what did it matter? I'd stay at Devereux long enough to save some money, get good references, and then find another job among more congenial people.'

'Hey,' Lucian said, sounding not surly, or smart aleck, but oddly shy, 'did you mean that about lending me some money? I'll pay you back as soon as I can earn it, honest.'

'I believe you,' I said. 'And yes, I do mean it.' I looked at him a long minute. 'You *will* go out to join your father, won't you?'

He flushed with anger but said, 'I guess I can't blame you for having doubts. But yes, I'll go. He and I get along pretty well. I'd have asked him for the fare before, but I'm only just sixteen, and there was a lot of custody flak. Anyway, if he'd sent me a money order, I wouldn't put it past Mom to open any letter from him to me. She's done it before.'

'What'll you do when you get there'

'Get a job with him or on a ranch. Like I said, the horses aren't so snobby, and I have worked around here so I know the ropes.'

'The horses aren't snobby at all. They don't care about their pedigree—or the pedigree of the people who ride them. The only ones who carry on about that are the idiot people around them.'

'True. I guess you know that if Mom catches on that you lent me the money, she'll really have it in for you.'

'That's fine. As I told you, I can produce a few items on her that she won't like at all.' I thought for a minute. 'Jeremy's going into town tomorrow. He'll have to use the stable car, but I'll steal a ride with him and bring you back the cash.'

'Thanks. I mean it. Thanks a lot.'

'You're welcome.' I held out my hand. To my surprise, Lucian leaned forward and kissed me on the cheek. 'Too bad I'm not older,' he said with his old derisive grin.

'I'm just as glad. I don't need trouble with you, too. By the way, can you wait until I've left before you take off?'

'Sure. I would anyway.'

Any faint hope I might have had that it would pour with floods of rain the week of Burwell—nothing short of a typhoon would halt the show—was about as realistic as most such hopes. The sun shone, there was a slight breeze, and the weather forecast was excellent. The only unexpected thing was Penelope's revelation that she had entered Nancy in a class that was showing on the Tuesday instead of Wednesday. That meant we had to get ourselves and our horses over there a day early, and there was a day's less instructing for Nancy.

'Never mind,' I reassured her. 'You'll do fine just as you are.'

Fortunately, Burwell was near enough so that we could take the horses over in the trailers early in the morning and bring them back in the evening. When we entered the enormous grounds at ten on Tuesday morning, my first impression was that there was room for hundreds of horses and vans and for thousands of people.

My second impression was that I was right: I *had* been to this enormous and important show before, and I could, at that moment, have drawn a map of the rest of the grounds.

Jeremy, Nancy and I had come in a car, pulling a horse trailer containing Bayou. John was coming later, bringing his horse, Malaya, and Penelope was driving her car. We found a wide, grassy spot for our van, and Nancy and I got out immediately to see how Bayou had fared in his travels. Like the steady, patient, wise horse he was, he had fared well, nibbling a thread or two of hay from the bundle swinging to one side of his van. The moment Nancy and I led him out, he discovered the grass, and we let him nuzzle it a moment or two before we started grooming him.

Weeks later, when I looked back on that

strange, and in many ways frightening day, I saw it as a series of pictures, small shots leading up to the events that, for the second time in my life, split apart my world.

With Bayou groomed and ready to be saddled, nibbling a bit here and there while Jeremy sat reading his paper beside him, Nancy and I went off to see the other parts of the show.

There were the usual classes going on, with judges either standing in the middle of a field or up in a stand, and the voices over loudspeakers announcing riders by number and, at the end of the classes, the names of the winners and their horses. It was, on the whole, a happy crowd, divided into a small group of contestants, in navy blue jackets, tight pants, and hunting caps, and the larger number of spectators in jeans, shirts and, frequently, straw cowboy hats—because the sun was hot. The leading trainers were very much in evidence, beside the rings, at the schooling area, giving contestants last-minute counsel, checking reins, saddles, girths.

'Who's that?' Nancy asked at one point. 'I've seen his picture somewhere.'

'That's Julian Mercer,' I said, astonished that I could identify the authoritative middle-aged man talking to one of the judges.

'He's supposed to be one of the best riders

in the country,' Nancy said. 'Mother showed me pictures of shows and he was in a lot of them.'

Did I know him, I wondered? Or did I just know who he was?

Nancy's first and easier class was to take place around eleven-thirty. So we went back to the trailer, put a bridle and saddle on Bayou, and walked him over to the schooling area.

It was while I was standing on the side, watching Nancy take Bayou over the jumps and calling out encouragement, that I suddenly heard John's voice beside me.

'Hello,' he said.

I turned. He, too, was wearing a navy blue jacket, which emphasized his lean waist and strong shoulders. 'She's riding well,' he said evenly. 'You're to be congratulated.'

I stared up at him, and in a second was horrified to feel a swelling in my throat. His eyes did not have that distancing look that I so hated and feared. They seemed, if anything, sad. How handsome he was, I thought, with his tan skin against the white stock! Why was I almost in tears about it?

Then I remembered his voice, rebuking me publicly for running after him. And I also remembered Ransom, whom he had ordered to be put down.

'Why did you have to kill him?' I asked.

He looked startled. 'Who?'

'Ransom.'

There was a silence. Then, 'Because it was the best thing to do.'

'It wasn't. He was a wonderful horse. You only did it because...because...'

'Because why?'

'Because Estes Conrad ordered you to, or he told Penelope to, to protect himself. Or she told you to, to protect Estes. Everybody cared about protecting everybody else and themselves— except not about protecting Ransom.'

I wanted so much for him to deny it.

Instead, he said, 'Why is Anson Grant looking at you so hard? Do you know him?'

'Who?' Silently, I was still pleading with him to tell me he was innocent of Ransom's death. But then a queer, convulsive shiver went through me. 'Who did you say?'

But at that moment Nancy rode up. 'Perdita —hadn't we better go over to the ring? Hello, John.'

'Hello, Nancy. You're riding very well. Just shows what you can do with a good teacher.'

'Oh, well.' She grinned. 'I guess I was just scared of you.'

'I'm sorry,' he said. 'I'm thinking of applying for a new personality.'

Nancy giggled. 'Shall we go over, Perdita?'

I was still trembling. Something strange was happening to me. But I felt this was Nancy's day, and I had to concentrate on supplying calm and reassurance.

Nancy breezed through her Novice class with no trouble and a lot of poise and confidence, winning herself second place.

'Terrific,' I said, when she came out of the ring.

'I'll show it to Mummy,' she said, with satisfaction.

Leaving Jeremy snoozing beside the relaxing Bayou, John, Nancy and I had lunch in the big lunch tent.

'Where's Penelope?' I asked.

'Off with some of her friends.'

'Mummy knows lots of people in the shows,' Nancy said, eating a hamburger with more gusto than she'd shown at meals at Stanton since I'd known her.

'Aren't you hungry?' John asked me. He'd issued the invitation to Nancy and me. Nancy, of course, accepted immediately, and I went along with her because she needed to have me with her today—or so I told myself. Something, perhaps John's presence, was having an inhibiting effect on my appetite.

'I had a big breakfast,' I said.

Nancy paused, hamburger halfway to her mouth. 'No, you didn't,' she said.

'Don't contradict, Nancy. It's rude,' I said.

'Well, but you didn't.'

'Nancy!'

There was a silence for a while.

'When is your class?' I asked John.

'Later this afternoon. Around four.'

'Working Hunter?'

'Yes.'

'John's won lots of ribbons,' Nancy said, wiping up tomato ketchup with the remains of her bun.

'You'll soon be doing better,' John said.

'You're *much* nicer than you used to be,' Nancy said.

'Thank you,' John said. 'One tries.' He glanced at me.

It suddenly struck me that Nancy was entirely right. John was displaying none of the tension, irritability and general ill humour that I had seen so often in him.

'Perhaps you're in love,' Nancy said thoughtfully.

To my great shock John turned bright red. 'That'll be enough,' he said. 'Remember what they used to say about children. They should be seen and not heard. I'll lock you in your room and feed you on bread and water.'

'Pooh!' Nancy said.

'You're getting awfully brave,' I said. I was still thinking about John blushing like that. If it meant what I thought it meant...'You've never talked back to John like that.'

'I'd never won two prizes before,' she said simply.

There was something rather pathetic and appealing in that statement. I was thinking of a reply when John forestalled me.

'You know,' he said, 'I don't like you just because you won prizes and proved you could ride. I like you anyway. You're my little sister, and I'm fond of you.'

'Then why were you so cross?'

'Because I thought maybe you were being forced to do something you didn't want to do—ride. I obviously didn't go about it the right way, but I was trying to rescue you. How could I know you're turning out to be a terrific horsewoman?'

'Hear, hear!' I said.

We were silent for a while. John was drinking coffee, Nancy had gone off to get herself some ice cream, and I was nibbling what remained of my salad.

Suddenly I said, 'Who's Anson Grant?' And could feel myself beginning to shake again.

'The man who was staring at you. Didn't you see him?'

'No. I was busy watching Nancy. Who is he?'

'Anson Grant,' John said, pouring himself some more coffee from the urn and stepping back to the table, '—otherwise known as Sonny—is Ann Devereux's manager and current boyfriend. All the local gossip says it's serious. He's rather known for cultivating rich ladies. Used to be married to Fiona Denbeigh, another rich woman, widow of an Englishman, Sir Peter Denbeigh. She, Fiona, had a daughter, so I'm told, by her first husband, who mysteriously disappeared about a year or so after her mother's death....' John had been glancing over toward the field where a group of ponies was being herded for a children's ring. Then, when I didn't say anything, he turned back. 'Perdita—is something the matter?'

I could feel the sweat on my body and the nausea in my mouth. My head was both throbbing and aching.

'Perdita—what is it? Darling—are you all right?'

He reached out and held my hands and I looked into his eyes. I knew then, that however strange his actions had been, there was some explanation. He couldn't be cruel or greedy. He was a decent, honest person and I loved him. And all the while I was recognizing this, I knew something else was going on in me, but I didn't know what it was. I felt queer, disoriented.

'John—let's take a walk. I feel strange.'

'All right. Are you sure you don't want me to get you something?'

I shook my head.

'Do you want me to take you back to Stanton?'

'No. I can't go back. I have to be here. You know how Nancy is. I'll be all right.'

'If you're not well, Nancy'll have to manage without you.'

'No. Let's walk. It may be sunnier outside, but there's also a breeze.'

Nancy had gone off to see Bayou and prepare for her second class. I was filled with an overwhelming anxiety—as though I were looking for something, but not only did I not know where to look, I didn't know what I was looking for. Maybe, I thought, John was right. Maybe I should get back to Stanton, which, at the moment, seemed like a haven. But some stubborn centre within me refused to do so. 'It'll be all right,' I muttered to myself, not realizing I was saying it aloud.

John pulled my hand through his arm and held it. 'You're right. It will be.'

For a moment my own nightmare receded. I smiled a little. 'What about all those threats Penelope—and Estes—were making at you?'

'Thanks to Estes' going on another bender and making a public ass of himself, nothing's going to come of them. He tried to show who was boss with one of the Devereux horses and got shipped off in nothing flat to a drying-out place. He's a cousin of Ann's, and she wasn't putting up with any of it.'

'What about that threat Penelope has over you?'

'Well, without her boyfriend Estes, she's a little hamstrung. They were perfect for each other. She's socially ambitious, and he wanted to lord it over his own stable. So they set out to try to oust me. When I wouldn't sell, she tried other methods—not paying bills, spreading damaging stories, and the night I beat up that friend of Lucian's I certainly played into her hands.'

'Why did you do it?'

'Because he and Lucian were strung out on something and he was playing with matches around one of the horse's stalls—he'd also been abusing the horses. I almost killed him, and I'm not as penitent about it as I should be, probably. He'll live to make some other creature miserable.'

'What a pity it was a kid. You know how courts are about that.'

'This kid, who was seventeen, was six-three and weighed thirty pounds more than I did.'

'Was that the same kid who started the fire?'

'It was Lucian who started the fire. No, the fire came after that with one of Lucian's pool hall buddies from the town. Unluckily for me, the father of the kid I beat up is an officer of the bank who holds the farm mortgage. He's a powerful citizen around here. The kid told his father he got drunk on beer and fell out of the hayloft on top of the barn. I guess he wasn't too anxious to tell the truth, either, about smoking dope and so on. And I certainly wasn't. At the least the father could have been ornery about the farm, and at the worst charged me with assault.'

'But could he send you to jail?'

'I don't know. The kid had some broken bones and lost teeth. I was half out of my mind with fury when I thought of what a fire could do to the horses. He was certainly in the hospital a while. And on my side there was only my word as to what the boy was doing. Lucian would tell any story his mother told him to save his own skin. I guess I felt the nets closing around me, with the tales Penelope was spreading, the debts, the way she was draining off all the money—everything. I'm sorry. It's not an excuse for the way I treated you...I just couldn't...couldn't cope with anything more.'

I squeezed his arm and he smiled down at me.

'Is he still a threat to you? The banker's son? Or has Penelope relented?'

'Not willingly. But she was undercut by her good friend, Estes. It seems that in his drunken exaltation he splatted to everyone at some gathering all the details of what he and Penelope were going to do with Stanton, once I was out of the way and it was theirs. Which wouldn't have gone over very well under the best of circumstances. You don't do that kind of thing. But by this time, people knew what he'd done to Ransom, so they weren't having any and simply turned their backs. And along with Estes', Penelope's credit and reputation, such as it was, was pretty much blown.'

'How do they know about Ransom?'

'People talk—probably the vet. And then with Estes getting drunk and trying to get rough with one of the Devereux horses, the whole thing came out.'

'But the vet was Matthew's friend—and you

said Matthew wasn't any friend of Stanton.'

'Matthew is a hanger-on, a gofer, a younger Estes without, at the moment, the drinking. You know the horsey world is a wonderful place for the socially upwardly mobile to find a foothold. If you're presentable and can ride you can go far—if that's what you want. Anyway, the vet would not feel inhibited by Matthew's calculations.'

I felt a little better as the afternoon wore on. The extreme dizziness and anxiety receded. When it was time to go and get Nancy and Bayou, John and I started across the long green meadow, brilliant in the afternoon sunshine.

'What's happening over there?' I pointed across where, past a line of trees and up another hill, more horses with older riders were competing.

'The outside Course. I'll be riding in there in another class in about an hour.'

I was staring at the distant field, across the incredible green carpet of the near one, when it happened.

A bay horse was being led up, on my left, cutting across us, about fifty yards away. I saw the black mane and fine head. Then, 'That's Band...Band...Bandeau,' I said, and knew that it was the wrong name. 'Not Bandeau...*Bandit*.'

291

'Bandit,' I yelled.

The horse, which was being led, jerked its head and then let out a whinny.

'Bandit!' I broke into a run.

The horse suddenly jerked itself harder and tugged its rein from the person leading it. Then, reins dangling, it came trotting towards me. I ran towards it. Pictures were going through my mind, of me and this horse, riding across other meadows, refusing to let someone take the horse, of a man's hand trying to force me to yield up the reins.

'Perdita!' Dimly I heard the shout behind me, but I ran on. I was a still a few yards from Bandit when suddenly I saw a big black horse coming rapidly towards me from the side. I turned. Anson Grant...Sonny Grant and I stared at one another and something exploded in my mind as the past and the present rushed together. I knew who he was, and he knew that now, at last, I knew.

'You killed my mother,' I said to Anson Grant, my stepfather. 'And then you tried to kill me.'

I saw the power I had felt across the restaurant turn into the blind rage I now remembered. His hand with the crop came down on the horse's flank. The horse plunged forward and then reared, blotting out Anson's face, just as in the dream I had had so often. And I was once again falling down...down...down...down the dark well.

The last thing I knew before I blacked out was my own name.

EPILOGUE

Some weeks later John and I were watching Nancy school Bayou through his paces in the ring. Ransom, looking much improved, was cantering around the paddock above the ring, pretending he was a colt.

'Why did you let me believe Jeremy's story about your having Ransom put down? And why didn't he tell me the truth?'

'He probably thought you'd get upset and blab the truth and then Estes would go and get him back. Not that you'd want him to, but you might give him a piece of your mind. You're not backward about that, you know.'

We grinned at each other.

'Is the stock now yours?'

'Mostly—including Ransom. Ann Devereux helped me to arrange to buy him. I was able to get a decent mortgage from another bank in town and buy out Penelope. I think when Estes went off his rocker and everyone knew of her connection with him, she decided to move to greener pastures. But I'm glad she left Nancy. Even though my claim to her as a stepbrother is pretty weak.'

'Nancy would have run away—she made that clear—if her mother had taken her away from Stanton and Bayou. And you. Sorry to put you last, but I think you rank third. Certainly after Bayou. And I think that's the reason Penelope left her. If Nancy had taken off, there would have been another scandal, and I suspect Penelope felt her social ambitions wouldn't have survived that. Anyway, Nancy has to go off to school in a week or so, and there's no reason she shouldn't spend the rest of her vacations here.'

John glanced at me. 'And what about you? Have you decided what name you're going to use? Perdita Smith or your real one, Prudence Denbeigh? Not that you're lost anymore.'

'I like Perdita, and I think I'm going to use that. I never really liked Prudence—maybe because it was the name of my least favourite godmother. I can live without Smith, not that I have any objections to it. It's a perfectly good name. But so is my father's—Denbeigh. So, I'll be Perdita Denbeigh.'

'Do you remember everything now?'

'Yes. Mostly. There are still gaps. But almost everything.' I paused, because so much that I remembered was painful.

'Until my father's death,' I said, 'my life was

pretty happy. My father was wonderful, gave me my first pony, taught me how to ride, taught me to love horses. We used to spend part of our time there, in Yorkshire, and part here in the States, in Connecticut. Then Daddy died. The place over there was sold and we came here permanently, and not too long after that, Mother met Anson....

'I don't know why but I hated him almost from the beginning. He looked at me in a funny way. But Mother was madly in love. You and Matthew and everybody else who described him were right: he had an incredible ability to make people—women—fall in love with him. And so he and Mother were married. I went to boarding school. But there were vacations ...and they were pretty awful. Anson was terribly sweet to me, giving me presents and so on, but in a way that made me uncomfortable— as though he wanted something, or was weighing how I would react. One day he sort of pulled my arm and tried to...to...to kiss me. This was right after giving me a bracelet. And Mother walked in. Anson suddenly pushed me away and told me I shouldn't do that kind of thing.

'When he left the room Mother went for me. She said it was disgusting in a child my age leading him on that way, that he'd spoken to her about it before. She was furious. I couldn't believe she'd say things like that to me. I tried to explain, but it didn't do any good. She absolutely adored him. She never felt that way about Daddy, I'm positive. Anway, I ran away for a while—to another horse farm, smaller than ours and much less organized, but nice. Then Mother came to get me. I knew I ought to confront her—make her listen to me. But I never did—I couldn't. And she didn't want to talk about it, either. She just said she hoped I wasn't going to go about telling silly stories. I said I was much too ashamed to.

'And the funny thing was, I *was* ashamed. Even though I knew what she'd said—about me leading Anson on—was absolutely untrue, especially since I loathed him, the fact that she'd say that to me, made me feel like it *was* true... It's hard to explain.'

'You don't have to,' John said. 'The same happened here, about the bills. Even though I knew I wasn't delinquent—I had every reason to think the bills were paid by Penelope, since that was her job—still I felt like I was the cheat. Then what happened? I mean, how did you come to lose your memory?'

'Well, I had one more vacation at home, and I stayed out of the house as much as possible. I'd bought Bandit, with some money Daddy'd left me. He was terribly expensive, but I saw him at a show and wanted him more than anything in the world. I had to get Mother's permission, of course. But I think she was feeling bad about me, so she let me buy him. I pretty much spent the summer with him. I'd have slept in the stable if they'd let me. He was... is...a wonderful horse. He used to put his head over my shoulder and follow me around....' My voice seemed to give out.

'Well, don't cry, Perdita. You know that Ann Devereux, as soon as she was told the facts of the case, said you could have him. To be fair to her, she didn't know, when Anson gave her Bandit with his name altered a little—just for safety—that he'd simply taken over your horse.'

'It's funny, isn't it? It was Bandit who brought my memory back.'

'Bandit?'

'Yes. Ever since I'd first seen him at the Paddington show I kept feeling some kind of tie with him. And when I saw Ann Devereux schooling him, it didn't look to me like they were working *together*. Bandit kept acting like he wanted to get away. I think now he wanted to come over to greet me. And his name bothered me. It was close, but not exactly right. Anyway, when I saw him at the Burwell, I knew suddenly that his name was not Bandeau, but Bandit, and I called it out. Then Anson came at me again on his black horse, just as in my dream, and I missed the really exciting part because I was out cold.'

'Everybody missed it luckily. Anson just got himself and his horse out of there with the speed of light. He left the horse in the Devereux van, got in his car, went back to Devereux Farm and shot himself. I suppose he knew you'd spill the beans about his pushing you down a well. How did that happen, anyway?'

'I suppose, to be accurate, he didn't actually push me. He just caused me to fall. Mother and I always lived up in Connecticut. But just before she died she bought another stable in this part of the country, on the other side of the convent. I'd never seen it, but I came here about a year ago, a few months after I'd graduated from school, since it partly belonged to me anyway, and I brought Bandit. I thought I might ride him in some of the local fall shows. Anyway, I went out riding one of those balmy warm days in late autumn. Anson was there and he followed me. He caught up with me when I was lying on the grass half asleep with Bandit grazing nearby. I hadn't tethered him, just loosened his saddle and taken off his bridle. I woke up, saw Anson coming across the field towards me, and got Bandit's bridle back on. But not in time. Anson came up, got off his own horse, and before I could get up on Bandit, got hold of me and started making passes. I clung to Bandit's reins, but he forced them out of my hand. I fought him off and told him what I thought of him and said—I suppose stupidly—that if he ever came near me again, I'd tell everybody what kind of person he was. I knew I'd made a mistake the moment I was finished. A queer look came over his face—not unlike the look he had when he almost rode me down in the show. And he started to beat me. He kept beating me and beating me and beating me, all the time yelling I'd led him on. I kept backing and trying to get away. Somehow I must have tripped over the rim of the well, kicking aside the half-rotten cover. And then, as he hit me again, I fell down into it....

'Since he's had the good sense to shoot himself, I don't suppose I'll ever know what he did then. But I gather he took Bandit back, and claimed he'd found him, riderless, and looked everywhere, but didn't find me. Then, later, he'd said I'd walked back and come straight to the house and left, almost immediately, for Connecticut. At least that's what I've been able to piece together from talking to the stable people and the police. After that, he simply said

I was away, and since there wasn't any more family, nobody was close enough to bother to look. Everybody knew I had relations in England, and he usually said I was there. That's one of the problems about living in two countries. I was always moving back and forth and never really had long-term friends anywhere. And then after Daddy died and before Mother married Anson, she and I used to go to the shows in Florida in winter.... It was easy for him. I was never really a missing person... which is why I wasn't on any list with the police or anybody like that.'

'Wouldn't there have been inquiries from banks—I mean, you inherited from your mother when she died, didn't you?'

'Yes. I got half the property—the house in Connecticut, and half the stock and the cash, and half the revenue from the stable here. But he was also appointed executor. So I suppose he could have fudged any questions anybody would have asked.'

'But wouldn't somebody smell a rat after a while?'

'Yes, and we'll now never know what dodge he was planning to use. He was always a gambler. That's something that used to upset Mother. I see now that it was probably the most essential part of his character...he gambled on everything: on Mother not believing me, on Ann Devereux not finding out about Bandit, on my not recognizing him at the restaurant, on being able to tuck me away at some other Devereux farm where I'd be safely remote from suddenly knowing who he was, on Mother's being killed in that accident and not him. I'll swear he stage-managed that, although I'll never be able to prove it.'

'How did she die—and when?'

'In a car accident, about a year and a half ago. She and Anson were coming home from dinner late one night and crashed into a truck. He got out with some scratches and bruises, but she was killed.'

'Well, what makes you think he arranged it?'

I paused a minute, remembering that last night I'd seen my mother. Finally, 'Because it was so convenient,' I said slowly. 'He and Mother had had a flaming row that day. I could hear them although I couldn't hear what they were saying. He was just back from California where he'd gone to look at some horses. But on the way he'd stopped at Las Vegas and lost a lot of money. I didn't know all the details, and I won't ever now. But the night she was killed she came into my room to say goodnight. She was all dressed for the dinner and looked beautiful. But she also looked distraught—I'd never seen her that way before. I asked her what the matter was. Mother said, "I think Anson lost a lot of money in Las Vegas. He didn't buy those horses. He used the money to gamble." Then she burst out. "He lied about it—said something about the horses not coming up to scratch and his putting the money down on some others. But a dear friend—the kind that's always eager to bring that type of news—just called and said she saw him out there at one of the gaming places with that actress he knows."

'She sat down on my bed then, and just stayed there, staring. Then she said, "Oh God, Pru, if you were right about him all along, I've done you a terrible injustice. We'll talk about it tomorrow. I'm sorry, my darling, I'm sorry .... I've made up my mind—" and at that moment I saw Anson in the doorway. Then they went out to that party and she was killed. It could have been an accident, but I don't believe it. He was driving, and when he tried to pass a trailer truck, crashed into it. He said the trucker deliberately veered out. But the trucker claimed that Anson cut back in too sharply, so that the person in the passenger seat—Mother—was crushed. There was nothing to say who was telling the truth. And there was no way the police could verify either story. Afterwards, the lawyer told me that Mother'd called him that afternoon and said she wanted to discuss divorce proceedings. But that night she was dead. So Anson inherited half of Mother's money and remained executor. He gambled again, and won.'

'Well,' John said, 'He gambled once too often. He gambled you were dead at the bottom of that well, and you weren't. It must have given him a nasty turn when he discovered that. How did he find out?'

'By sheer luck—from his point of view. Matthew took pictures of Nancy and Bayou and me at the Paddington Show. He said something about being the official Devereux photographer, so he was going around with his camera. Obviously Anson saw the picture. What Matthew told me afterwards was that he'd explained how well Nancy had performed and that it was all due to my fine instruction, and was kind enough to add that Anson was always interested in a pretty girl—'

'Not kind—truthful,' John said, and smiled. Then he kissed me lightly. 'Quite truthful.'

It was a minute before I could get my breath back.

'So,' John said, 'he saw that you were back from the dead and concocted some story for Matthew about wanting to hire you. What do you think was going on in his mind? How could he know that you'd lost your memory?'

'I think it was another of his gambles. I figure he argued to himself that if I hadn't lost my memory, why hadn't I come to get him with blood in my eye?'

John rubbed his nose. 'Of course, you might not have known he was at Devereux. On the other hand, if everything was clear sailing, you'd have surfaced with your real name, Prudence Denbeigh, wouldn't you? In other words, the fact that you showed up over a year after your mother's death, and months after you fell down the well, bearing a different name, would certainly be strange enough to make him think something had happened.'

I nodded. 'So, he took his gamble—egged Matthew on to try and hire me, and then, in his most supreme gamble, let me see him at that restaurant.'

'I'll say this for him,' John said, 'he had nerve beyond nerve. If you'd taken one look in that restaurant and been shocked into remembering, it would have been curtains for him with Ann Devereux.'

'Would it? Wouldn't it have been just the story of another hysterical girl who'd lost her head over him? I mean, after all, he managed to turn my own mother against me. Couldn't he deal with a woman who was already in love with him and without any interest in crediting what I had to say? Isn't it what rejected girls always do? Make up wild accusations about men who had only meant to be fatherly and kind? It's hypothetical now, but I bet you that if I had come around at the Burwell and confronted him, he would have had an explanation for everything I accused him of, and what's more, it'd be an explanation that would have made me look silly.'

'If that's the case, why did he lose his head at the show? I was there, Perdita, and saw his face. He wanted to murder you. If he'd had his way, that big stallion of his would have trampled you into jelly.'

'Because I think for one thing I caught him by surprise. Penelope only entered Nancy for those shows on Tuesday at the last moment. Or if she'd done it before, she only told Nancy and me at the last minute. I'd told Matthew we were going to be there Wednesday. Anson had probably arranged not to be there on Wednesday, but wasn't expecting to see me Tuesday. So it was a shock. And I think that he'd never gotten over his rage at some of the things I'd flung at his head the last time I'd seen him. They weren't calculated to flatter his considerable male ego, and I believe that with the shock, his fury broke through. Also maybe he knew that the jig was up—that no matter how many plausible lies he told, sooner or later people would know the truth, that there were too many lies already. Always before I'd guess he felt that he could bluff, charm, lie, or flatter his way through anything. At that moment at the Burwell when he saw me, and knew that I recognized him, I think the balance tipped the other way, and he knew the old methods wouldn't work for him any longer. I don't know. Now that he's dead, we'll never really know for sure.'

We didn't say anything for a moment, then John said, 'It was Anson who ran you down that night after you'd been to see Reverend Mother Julian, wasn't it?'

'Yes. He used the old station wagon that belonged to the farm, not knowing that Matthew had used it when we had gone out together—or maybe, who knows? he hoped to pin it on Matthew. I don't think he would shrink from a little thing like that.'

'Pity. I was rather hoping it would turn out to be Matthew.' John said it so solemnly it took me a minute to realize he was joking.

'Come on,' I said. 'Why?'

'Jealousy.'

I grinned. 'I bet.'

John took my hand and held it. 'Why, according to what the police know, did he do it?'

'Well, when the police questioned Matthew, he repeated as much as he could remember of the conversation he and I had had on the phone immediately before I set out for the convent. In it, I'd said, among other things, that large parts of my memory were coming back. The really funny part is that when we hung up, or rather just before, I heard a click, and thought to myself, 'Oh that's Penelope, up to her old listening games again,' completely forgetting that Penelope was away on a business trip. On the way to the convent, and on the way back, before Anson bashed into me, I had a vague feeling that I'd got something wrong...that there was something I should be paying attention to, but couldn't push whatever it was from my unconscious to my conscious mind. Well, it was the fact that since Penelope wasn't there, the listener had to be at Matthew's end. If I had been able to figure that out, I still wouldn't have known it was Anson, because this was before the crucial parts of my memory had come back. But afterwards, after Anson shot himself and I could remember most of the past, the police figured it was Anson who heard me say that I was remembering much more, and who therefore took the most direct means to ensure that I wouldn't be remembering any further.'

'You'd have thought he'd find some car that had nothing to do with anyone at Devereux.'

'Maybe, if he'd had time, he would have. But I think he acted on impulse, which, of course, has always been part of his pattern. He was a terrific con man, but he wasn't a master planner. In the couple of days between the car crash and the Burwell, the police were able— from my description of the car—to trace it to the old station wagon at Devereux. Matthew, apparently, has been the one to use it most, but when they discovered he spent the entire evening in the stables in full view of half a dozen other people, they were beginning to make other inquiries. Then, after the Burwell, it became fairly obvious that it must have been Anson.'

'How much do you think Matthew knew— about the real reason for Anson's interest? I'm not crazy about him for a lot of reasons, but he isn't stupid. He surely must have know Anson's motive was more than just acquiring another pretty girl. You've seen him since, haven't you?'

'Once. He came over here to apologize profusely for any share he had had in Anson's plans and to tell me over and over again that he simply thought Anson was doing his usual number when he saw a pretty girl he wanted to have around the place.'

'Do you believe him?'

'Not entirely. I doubt that he had any idea who I was or what Anson had done to the mysteriously missing Prudence Denbeigh. But he's the kind of man who wouldn't care, who, if he could be useful to the boss, wouldn't look too carefully at what the boss's motives were. Which I think is almost as rotten as if he did know.'

John, who had not let go of my hand, stood looking down at it, as though he were thinking of something else. Then he said, 'This whole lost memory thing is very weird. I take it it was all caused by the blow to your head when you fell down the well. But what brought it back all of a sudden?'

'Well, I talked to my old neurologist—the one who put me through all the tests and asked all the questions when I was still at the convent. He said he's always thought that although the blow to my head caused my loss of memory of what happened immediately before I fell, that there was a strong psychological element, too, blocking the return. And what it was was the shock and horror of having Mother turn against me, of believing Anson when he said

311

I'd tried to seduce him rather than believing me. I told you that even though I knew there wasn't a word of truth in it, the fact that she refused to believe me made me feel guilty. Then, when he started the whole thing all over again after her death, it was a sort of terrible replaying of the accusation. And after I'd tried to push him away and called him some ugly names of my own, he started making the same accusations against me as he was beating me up, as he had before. So I just blocked the whole thing out, and kept it blocked for nearly a year. It's funny, I think that's one reason I resisted having my picture taken at the Paddington. On some deep level, unconsciously, I didn't want to do anything that might open up the past. Everybody—the nuns and doctors—kept saying, ''Try to remember the past.'' But of course I didn't want to—so I didn't.'

'And taking a picture of you would do that for you—open up the past?'

'It might. Somebody might recognize it. And that's exactly what happened. Anson recognized it, and set the whole machinery in motion that led to the confrontation at the Burwell.'

'What finally kicked the door open to let the memory back in?'

'It felt sudden, but I'm not sure it was—at least that's what the doctor I saw last week said.

312

It was partly just the passage of time, he said, that I was readier to face things.... I was surer of myself....' I paused and glanced at John. 'There was something else, something I didn't tell the doctor..... That day at the Burwell, at lunch, when you and I were alone...' I paused and took a deep breath. 'I suddenly knew how I felt about you. I knew that though you might be bad-tempered and free with your fists, I loved you and could trust you to the ends of the earth.... This is not an official medical opinion, understand,' I added with mock gravity. 'But that's what I think. What I felt about you gave me courage to look at what had happened. So, when Anson rode up on his horse, the whole thing came back in a huge wave.'

John leaned over and kissed me. 'I'm glad,' he said simply.

For a fully occupied moment we didn't say anything. Then I pulled away a little. 'There's just one weird thing, though.'

'What?'

'Well, when Anson came riding up on his black stallion, it was just like the dream I'd had several times. There was this huge black horse, rearing up, blotting out the sky, its hooves above my head....' My voice faded a little as the dream came back in all its vividness.

'Well, isn't that what happened when he beat

you up at the well? He came riding up on his horse?'

'But it wasn't a black horse, and anyway, he tethered it, before walking over toward me. No, what I kept dreaming happened, but it happened *after* I dreamed it.'

John looked at me thoughtfully. 'Maybe you're psychic. Some philosophers say that time is simply another dimension, like space, that we happened to be in, but that outside of time the past and the future are the same.'

'Oh.' I tried to envision it and failed.

'Speaking of the future, what are you going to do?'

'Well...Mother Julian thinks I ought to go to the college as I had planned to.'

'Do you want to?'

I sighed. 'Not very much. I'd rather work with horses and go to college part time, if necessary.'

'You could work here. We could be partners...couldn't we?'

I looked at him. 'Why did you push me away that time and put me down in front of all those people? You were *horrible* to me.'

'I thought for sure Penelope'd carry out her threat and I'd find myself in jail or at least in bad trouble, and everything seemed pointless and stupid. I couldn't see any future—for us,

314

anyway—at all. Pushing you away seemed the greatest favour I could do you. And putting you down in front of other people—I knew you'd never forgive that. Besides, you were pretty horrible to me. You pushed *me* away. Remember?'

'I know. I didn't know *then* why I did that. I do now. It was the frightening thing the doctor said that was partly blocking me. I realized now that I confused it with something I couldn't remember—Anson coming after me right before I fell down the well. After that, without knowing why, I'd push anyone away. You understand now, don't you?'

'I'll understand if you'll understand.'

I put my hand on his shoulder. He put his over mine and pulled me to him. 'When I said partners, I sort of had something more permanent in mind, too. After all, you're eighteen now. You're grown up.'

'That's right. I am. Mostly.'

'Well,' he said, and kissed me. 'What do you think about it?'

'I think I'd like to think about it, quite seriously,' I said, and kissed him back.